I0659121

PHANTOM
DRIFT

A JOURNAL OF NEW FABULISM

ISSUE 10: *Tenth Anniversary Issue*

Phantom Drift Limited   Issue Ten
Portland, Oregon   Fall, 2020

PHANTOM DRIFT
A Journal of New Fabulism

Editorial Board

Matt Schumacher, Managing Editor
Nate Liederbach, Fiction Editor
Tom Weller, Fiction Editor
Ilana Darrant, Fiction Editor
Elizabeth Schumacher, Poetry Editor
Mary Bond, Poetry Editor
John Morrison, Poetry Editor
David Memmott, Editor Emeritus
Lesley What, Editor Emeritus
Martha Bayless, Editor Emeritus

ISSN: 2162-8211
ISBN: 978-0-9964426-5-7

Design & Layout: *Kristin Summers, redbat design*

Issue Ten Cover Art: *"Candy Forest" by Nicoletta Ceccoli (2012, acrylic on paper, 21" x 18")*

Phantom Drift Limited is a 501(c)(3) tax-exempt organization founded to develop an understanding of and appreciation for fabulist literature. *Phantom Drift* is one of the few literary journals in the United States focused on fabulist writing. We aim to nurture the literature of fabulism, the fantastic, and the surreal by publishing an appealing, top-quality literary journal featuring only the best short stories, poetry, and critical thinking on fabulism by established, emerging, and new writers from the U.S. and abroad. Our support for writers takes the form of not only providing a showcase for their works, but offering payment, a practice that both assures us the best of writers' work and supports literature as a whole. The journal will be published annually in the fall. Donations are deductible to the extent allowed by law. Orders, subscriptions and donations can be made on-line at www.phantomdrift.org.

Direct mail orders can be made by sending check or money order for $15 (postage paid) to:

Phantom Drift
8523 N. Curtis Avenue
Portland, OR 97217

Phantom Drift accepts on-line submissions from January 1 – April 30.

PHANTOM CROSSING

In a year when the most ludicrous conspiracy theory still managed to galvanize fanatics, when sureties like when we would return to work became impossible to guess, when bystanders could practically stand and watch the failed stimulus packages float by like stacked cumulus, *Phantom Drift* is still here for you, a tried and true bastion of fantastic literature, a dependable modern wunderkammer.

We suddenly find ourselves in our tenth year, and consequently, you hold in your hands a published anniversary issue. In the spirit of gala celebration, we would like to thank past editors, current editors, our designer, contributors, and audience. We also wish to express considerable gratitude for grants from both the Regional Arts and Culture Council and the Reser Family Foundation. Thank you one and all for your help and support in the last decade, for without you, *Phantom Drift* would not exist.

Whether you are seeking an escapist respite, or intent upon a full-frontal confrontation with the absurdities of the world, we're pleased to fulfill either need, and glad to bring you much satisfying strangeness in this issue. Feast your full sockets on "Candy Forest," the splendid cover art of Nicoletta Ceccoli, and the surrealist collages of Tudor Evans and Julia Lillard. Witness catastrophe and uncanny calm: the floods and fires of Rebecca Berg's "The Gray and the Orange," "The Rounding Hour" of Lesley Hart Gunn. Turn the page and gaze into the eyes of the strangest animals: let a thousand white cranes climb into your eye in Jenny Grassl's "Whiteness and the Alchemists," or observe as "The Seagulls" of Jacob Chapman's poem mysteriously take over a town. Be eyeballed by Daniel Ferris's "Ghoulfish." Glimpse the headless raven that may be hiding its head in its wings in Bruce McCallister's "The Bleeding Child Tarot." Take the time to hang out with the kids and Uncle Frank in Derek Annis's "Potato Salad." Don't forget to let your heartbeat reverberate with the strangenesses of technology: settle into the "pervasive dread" of Melissa Reddish's "Sanctity, Sanctuary," or the q (and no a) of Aaron Anstett's apostrophe-rich "Plea."

Were *Phantom Drift* a person in previous years, it might have been seen as a ringmaster of some surrealistic circus or a threshold guardian who kindly directed you to the wonderfully weird. Today, we and our mission are ever more urgent and necessary, for our authors and artists generate wonder and harness fear. Furthermore, we showcase the fantastic in an age that so needs the dreamiest of imaginations; such minds can show us, as Michael Stein writes in "The Flight of Icarus," "airy kingdom(s)...where prisons are an impossibility." *Phantom Drift* is at present a literary hideaway in trying times of uncertainty, a paginated escape from unemployment rates, and a Bachelardian shelter for the imagination during a season when there were so many hurricanes the weathermen ran out of names.

And we're glad you're here.

Matt Schumacher
Managing Editor
Phantom Drift

TABLE OF CONTENTS

FICTION

POETRY

✧ NON-FICTION/FEATURES

 DEREK ANNIS

POTATO SALAD

Growing up, the best part of summer
was the family picnic
in the public park, and the best part
of the family picnic was the appearance
of Uncle Frank, who chewed
the wet butts of cheap cigars
and wore prosthetic earlobes
where his eyelids
used to be. Each year,
he let us kids pick our favorite
dried leaf from his breast.
There were many leaves.
The selection process
took many hours.
Since I was the luckiest
of the kids, I always picked
the leaf with the most
ticks. The others scowled at me
in a display of profound
reverence. Uncle Frank and I
had a laugh at their expense,
and observed the family tradition
of bashing them with sticks.
Then, just as suddenly as he appeared
Uncle Frank was off again,
into the lake, waving goodbye
with his stone hands. *Goodbye,*
Uncle Frank! we said. *Goodbye, Frank!*

said the thousands of spiders
gliding gracefully down
from pine boughs overhead.

MELISSA REDDISH

SANCTITY, SANCTUARY

The noise comes at night, usually. Some say it is a tinkle while others a long, low peal. Everyone had expected a scream, a squelch, a faint buzzing like in a psychological thriller, but no, the noise was much more subtle than that. Regardless, Lace knows the drill. They reach quickly underneath their bed until their fingers find the box's wooden grooves. While some residents keep their boxes on their nightstand or even underneath their covers, Lace knows how easily a sprung clasp can seep out through the curtains and stain the entire neighborhood. What a pariah they would be, then!

Before Lace can register whether the noise is moving towards them or away, they reach up and pluck out a single eyelash. They slide the clasp of the box open, careful to keep the lid shut, and then with the quickest of gestures, open the lid and flick the eyelash inside. It doesn't matter where it lands. All that matters is that the eyelash is safely contained.

Lace listens for a moment, their head turned to the window. The noise is moving away. Well, better safe than sorry.

Lace slides the box back underneath the bed. They have to sneeze, but they stifle it. No need to attract unwanted attention. And then they remember their favorite book when they were little: a man with a sneeze so powerful, it wreaks havoc on the earth—causing earthquakes, toppling cities, even shaking the suits right off of rich businessmen. Each passerby tells the man to stop sneezing, but he shrugs his shoulders and says that he has very bad allergies. After everyone tries giving the man home remedies, each more outlandish than the last, a hundred hands grab the man and lock him inside a sound-proof cage. The man sneezes and sneezes (he is allergic to the metal bars) until he shakes the skin right off his body. Of course, the whole thing was very cartoonishly drawn, so the man was not a horrifying mound of blood and viscera but a goofy-looking skeleton with a shocked expression on his face. Still, the ending had frightened Lace so much that they had forced their mother to read it, over and over, night after night, a perverse repetition meant to weaken the book's terrible thrall but which had only increased it until the book became a kind of talisman: a severed foot, the bleeding just barely staunched, wrapped in gauze and jammed through a two-dollar keyring. Of course, Lace can no longer access that all-encompassing terror. This is probably a good thing.

We've always been wrong about the body—not just the slipstream outer layer but also that pulsing inner sanctum—though it wasn't until recently that we understood how wrong. Lace, like many other lost children, had listened with rapt attention to the glorified errors of the past. The humors—black bile, yellow bile, blood, and phlegm— explained by a woman so maudlin the class took to secretly calling her Bilious Barbara—and later, the notion of hysteria—wandering womb, nervous depression, and always the threat of the padded cell— all of it told in tones that were, quite frankly, hysterical. Back then, Lace was just happy to be called Lace. They barely registered the anomalies stacking up before them. By the time Lace graduated, they still didn't realize that each lecture was a series of minor treacheries intended to bruise. Once the trees began to weep black bile, that was when it was abundantly clear.

Though it is not advisable to spend much time outside, Lace needs groceries. On the way, they try not to glimpse the overgrown field with the worn-down path leading to its turmeric center. Today, the field has five bodies. Two men and three women. The bodies are hunched, mouth flush with the dirt, faces blank with the ecstasy of hoovering. What do they think about when they are in there? Lace doesn't know. Before, everyone was afraid the people would attach themselves to passing cars once the field ran fallow, but that hasn't happened. Still, it is better not to invite disaster. Lace glances once more before forcing their eyes back to the road, and that's when they see her. Carol-Lynn Miller. The neighbor who had stepped back, visibly shocked, when Lace had knocked on her door to say hello, be neighborly, with a curt *who are you* that Lace knew the woman meant to be *what*, not *who*. Lace can't stop the smile from zippering wide their face, the quiet schadenfreude of seeing the women here, like this. For a moment, just one moment, Lace sees a body stop its frantic hoovering and sniff the air. One Mississippi. Two Mississippi. But Lace is already gone, and so, the body returns, the O of its mouth finding in the dirt its perfect wet ring.

In the parking lot of Food Lion, Lace concentrates. The skin-prickling tang of the schadenfreude, the sweet-turned-bitter-turned-sweet lemonade that wets the inside of Lace's underwear—no, *stop*, not there—Lace loops and gathers in their mind until it is cotton-candy soft and pushes the sticky, delicious mess into the tip of their upper incisor. Do they put it there intentionally to make it unavailable? Perhaps. This feeling is for no one but them.

Lace is home, sanctity, sanctuary mere feet away, but they are so *tired* of being inside, so they walk to the backyard. The backyard dips in its very center like an illustration of gravity. Every time it rains, the backyard floods, and Lace finds various debris floating inside: candy wrappers, aluminum cans, broken toys, used condoms. Today, the very center of the backyard, the lowest point of the dip, has a two-foot square of liquid inside. The liquid is thick, viscous, yellowish-clear. It wobbles like jelly. Lace knows without touching exactly what it is. They look up at the sky, pink and throbbing. Oh no. There is a sound like a round of applause. Lace passes out.

Lace is inside a bar and they are drunk. Everything is dark and thrumming, and there are too many bodies pulsing like dying neutron stars. A whorl of green is a sudden buoy against the sweeping night. Is it a vision, tendrils of light like water wings amid darkness' deep, dense well? Or is just the cursive O of the Coors Light sign? Lace is staring half-lidded at an empty stool, envisioning a woman, willing that woman beaded clutch by lower back tattoo into existence, (women, after all, are safer) but their gravity well wasn't deep enough, because here he is, silver-tipped beard and cigarette smoke, his lips a perfect circle around Lace's throat, and Lace isn't sure if he is taking something or giving it away, but then again, isn't that every casual encounter, every fluttering gaze splayed and pinned in place, every open mouth an invitation to freefall?

Inside Lace's bed that now smells of cigarette smoke, Lace is thankfully alone. Time to still the sloshing waters. Time to rise and take stock. All body parts, secure. All existential crises, muted. Last night was an error, yes, one they will not be repeating. Lace knows to stay behind glass at all times, but they were tired, careless. It won't happen again.

Lace reaches under the bed out of instinct, even though they have no new castaways, but the box isn't where they left it. They reach around, their fear a fur-lined stole, and that is when they see it: open, tipped, empty. They grab the box and reach five fingers tentatively inside, trying to find a hint of detritus, an echo of bashful indignation. Nothing.

What if the man wasn't in the sound's thrall at all? What if he too was an O? Or worse, something entirely new?

Such pervasive dread is tricky to work with. It is a cold, gummy paste that sinks and sticks and spreads. Not easily corralled into a strand of hair or a single rolling teardrop. And Lace is exhausted from last night's round robin, so they are a failure of focus as well.

No matter. There is the rest of today, so long as the sky doesn't grow bleak with longing. The worst squall that Lace can remember is the day last March when the branches of the dogwood began scritch-scratching at their window, the hole at its gaunt center oozing pus. Lace had scrambled to fit the only mask they owned (a t-shirt strip, half a band name still visible) across their face. Then, a couple seconds later, the tree exploded into a million thrilling particles of white. Each one suctioned to the windowpane, fluid, undulating, before finally drifting off to infect the lungs and mind of the first lazy passerby.

Lace is about to strip their sheets when they catch sight of the clock—10:42—and remember that today is Saturday. Lace's shift starts at noon. Lace is not essential, but they are expendable, so after a quick change of clothes, it's back to the car for another exciting tour through life's bleak, suffocating hellscape.

Lace is inside the basement of a small storefront at the corner of Second and Carroll. They are stirring a large plastic tub with a modified plastic shovel. Inside the tub is a noxious mix of chemicals corrosive to anything alive. Overhead, an industrial fan purportedly sucks all of the fumes out, but still the room quivers with innuendo. Lace has learned not to breathe too deeply. They can take as many breaks as they like on the small square of asphalt out back, but it is an open, exposed space, so they hoard breath like a Sunday shopper and work for six-hour stretches. On a long wooden table puckered from careless droplets, small glass vials sit with plastic funnels at the ready. Each is lined with an essential oil and a different pithy name—Leave Him Lavender, Eucalyptus & Escape, Resting Rosehip. When the mixture is complete, Lace will pour a small scoop into each vial, screw a spray cap on each one, line them up on a plastic dinner tray from Goodwill, and ring the bell for a ferryman to deliver them upstairs. Customers hoping to temporarily halt whatever organism—protozoic, photosynthetic, passive-aggressive— is headed their way can spray a mist into the air. It won't incapacitate, but it will weaken or wound, which is theoretically enough time to escape (assuming you have somewhere to escape to). Lace knows the mixture doesn't work—everyone knows this—but it is better than sitting at home all day and gnawing your own leg off.

Lace's shift goes (and goes and goes) until each droplet is accounted for and the tub is sprayed down. Lace removes the layers of plastic on their head and chest and legs (but not, oddly enough, their arms) and wipes each carefully down. All they are feeling right now is a full-body fatigue. Such an offering would do nothing but enrage, so Lace has to hope they can stir up a more potent emotion on the ride home.

Even though such a move is reckless, Lace loops past the grocery store and slows when they reach the field. Today, there are seven bodies inside. Mrs. Miller isn't one of them, but he is. Lace can almost smell the cigarette smoke, even though their window is closed. The man from the bar stops suctioning the ground—his beard is whiter than Lace remembers—and stares straight at them. Lace wonders if he is feasting on their burnt offerings: the time when Lace was thirteen and raced their friends door-to-door trick-or-treating and the hot shame they felt when the woman who opened the first door asked: isn't Lace too old to be doing this sort of thing, still? Thirteen was the year that Lace had said fuck it to everything: dresses, curfew, homework, gender. It was the year they made out with Sandy Ingersoll and Lee Hoang on the same night. It was the year their mother had locked herself in her bedroom and threatened to jump out the second story window if Lace didn't calm down and start listening right this goddamn second. It was the year of the ripest emotions, the ones most easily plucked from their life's tree. And there in that burnished center, sun-ripened and wheat-soft, Lace could feel each moment wash golden across their body again. The memories were still there, yes, but without emotion they were sour, sterile things, not worth the headspace they were taking up. In exactly three gestures, Lace could be in that suffused space, cocooned in a panorama of youthful portents, each vision stuttering out that essential vowel: I, I, I.

That ought to do it. Lace hits the gas and drives home.

Nighttime. The hours of simple darkness, long past color and light. Lace has swept the longing tinged pink with nostalgia into ten different hair follicles and, snipping them one by one, placed them in the box. That should be sufficient for one night at least. Though naturally, tonight is quiet—no pressure that comes from an oncoming train, no deep reverberation at the end of a cymbal crash. Lace glances out the window, just to be safe, and that's when they see him. Again.

They walk away from the window, then return. He is still there. They could call the police, but what would they say? He is just standing there, hardly taking up space. And the police are a little busy with other matters.

When Lace returns to the window, the man is holding up a sheet of paper. It has a phone number on it.

Quietly, Lace creeps downstairs. They walk to the front door and touch the deadbolt, as though to make sure. Then they call the number.

"I know you can't let me in," the man says. His voice has the timbre of someone who smokes his own meats.

"No."

There is a pause, and for a moment, Lace thinks this will be their entire encounter. Then the man continues. "Would it help if I told you that I'm feeling better? More like myself?"

"Not really."

"Yeah," the man sighs, "I know. Better safe than sorry."

Lace touches the space where the door doesn't quite meet the frame. Though they can't see all the way through, they wonder if this is a weak spot, one the man could exploit. "Why are you here?"

"I was outside when I shouldn't have been. I just get so sick of being cooped up all the time. It ain't natural, the way we're living. Anyway, I went for a walk by the river to see the shipbuilders. Sometimes I can hear their music across the water and see that little spark of light from their torches. And it makes me feel, I don't know, less alone. But the shipbuilders weren't there, and then I saw that the water was lapping over the edge, and it wasn't exactly water, if you catch my meaning. And hoo boy, it had been a while. I really didn't even need much of a push. And then afterward, I found your box... I know it wasn't right, taking it like that, but I had been neglecting mine, and I didn't want to turn into one of them. Ironic, I know. I thought I could borrow a few, just to get me through the week, so I opened it, and well, Christ. It was... it was beyond anything I had ever felt. It was some metaphysical shit right there. I fell, fell hard, for you. Everything about you. So here I am, at your door, even though I'm probably the last jackass you want to see right now."

Lace hangs up the phone. So, this is what happens to those who return—they whip to and fro in their own emotional eddies until they can find a current strong enough to sustain them. Whoever the man was before all of this, he's lost all sense of division or propriety. They will not be joining hands again.

Lace checks to make sure that the curtain is closed, that the man is not trying to lay claim to more that isn't his, and then climbs back upstairs. They will not sleep tonight, but no one else needs to know that.

Sunday. At least Lace thinks it is Sunday. It is hard to tell and has been for a while. Lace peeks out the window: nothing but an empty slab of concrete. That is one benefit of their current situation: very few stoop hagglers now.

The breakfast burrito Lace heats in the microwave is limp with despair. Lace tries to wall off their thoughts, flatten each loop into a tidy square, but the man and his quivering beard keep intruding. Lace can't stop imagining the man plastered to their window, his bottomless O boring a hole through the glass. He climbs into Lace's bedroom, screws open Lace's head, and places rocks hand-selected from the quarry inside. Lace's head fills with limestone and dolomite, shards of shale. *Stay still*, the man whispers. *Don't you want to be a pretty, rattling thing?*

There is only one thing to do, but Lace doesn't want to do it. Their last clearing was over a year ago, and they just managed to fill out their edges again. But Lace is feeling unsafe, and that feeling is the most dangerous of all.

Lace prepares a space at the foot of their bed. They lay down the blanket their grandmother knitted for their mother, a totem that probably once held significance. They sit cross-legged and place one hand on each knee. They need to be alert but not anxious, loose but not too relaxed. Then they begin. The schadenfreude tucked deep within their upper incisor is the first they work out, tonguing the sticky sour sweetness one drop at a time. Next is the full-body tilt toward the smell of cigarette smoke followed by the brief and unsatisfactory orgasm. The next couple hours are spent in a glass-eyed focus, every secret stash flicked away then pushed to the tips of their toenails. In a final gesture that is funereal and slick with exhaustion, Lace clips their toenails to the quick, shaking their entire universe into the box.

Well, now that's done. They pull the laptop onto their bed and boot up a spreadsheet they had been putting off for a rainy day. As the computer trills a familiar tune, one that evokes no memories whatsoever, Lace stares unfocused at the window square—a pretty unbroken blue—before getting back to work.

Peter O'Donovan

TWO POEMS

PARASITE

I found another face had grown over mine.
A mask identical in all facets:
same sags, same lines, same bulging eyes
that always appear to be enclosing
something not quite contained, trying to escape.

He doesn't even seem aware of me,
this face that always gets the first word in,
interrupting, making bold conjectures,
or claims the first lick of sweet, leaving me
in aftertaste, at the back of the tongue.

The face does extremely well for himself,
accomplishing more than I ever did.
He networks feverishly, must be seen
at all the important parties, honing
his pitches, refining his credible smile.

Perhaps I am the parasite, latched on
from the inside, muttering my judgements,
bitter to no longer be heard at all,
while the face softens, developing jowls
to match his growing prestige and power.

Sometimes, I suspect there are others
even deeper than me, the sunken selves

I might have buried and then forgotten,
held together in a chain of faces,
all watching from within, all falling away.

SHOULD YOU CONSIDER A HOUSE MADE FROM LEAVES?

Long popular in Germany, leaf homes are at the center of new revival, a growing movement for sustainable living. This traditional eco-friendly material is carefully harvested in the summer, then woven in wide sheets that spiral conically upwards, reaching 50 meters or more. Far from the misconceptions about fragile structures, today's leaf homes provide unparalleled durability and resilience, and are able to withstand hurricanes, failed marriages and even regime change. Another common concern is fire resistance. However, the design of leaf homes funnels heat evenly throughout the structure; the smallest desire can warm the interior, while deadly fevers are easily dissipated within the curving walls. The distinctive winding hallways extend for miles inside the home, and suit a range of styles, from the contemporary to the melancholic. Some owners claim to have never seen the same room twice. Others that there is only one room, divided into a thousand fragments by sunlight flickering through the foliage. Assembling a leaf home can take as little as a lifetime, and once complete, can seem to disappear into the landscape. Wandering within, one might come across a mountain stream, or a humming marketplace, or even your dead, walking beside you, mouths moving with rustling sounds.

REBECCA BERG

THE GRAY AND THE ORANGE

When my city banished Revulo, I was in the kitchen. I was experimenting with yeast to see if I could recreate the pastries of my childhood: hamantaschen, popovers. Then I heard and stepped outside.

"*Revulo,* what kind of name is that, anyway?" people said.

I said I thought it might be Esperanto.

"Well, he or she wasn't related to us," they said.

I said Revulo knew how to build greenhouses. Solar panels. He'd fixed my window. Besides, what kind of city did we want to be?

"Easy for you to say," they said.

It was true I lived high up on the hill in the middle of town. My house was miles from the floods and fires nipping at the city. It was a small house, but it had a porch, a yard, and a view. I could watch storms approach. I could see militias and wild animals crossing the plains, and, even with binoculars, the texture of individual stones. Also, I was old. I didn't need a lot to eat. From my grandmother, I had inherited flour, oil, a little sugar, and a lifetime supply of yeast packets. I had fruit trees I'd planted decades ago. These things sufficed and were not too much; no one was interested in my apples and pears. They needed protein for their children. Wolves had been picking off livestock, even inside city limits.

"I realize," I said, "that I have no right to criticize."

"Nevertheless, you persist," they said, "in trying to make us feel bad."

* * *

Fog enveloped the city. This was just before or just after Revulo left—I don't remember which. It smelled of boiled eggs, burnt toast, and ozone. You could barely see your feet; buildings just looked like dark patches. Through the haze, from the fields burning outside the city, an occasional flicker was visible. Some of us wondered if the fog had caused the banishments. Or even if the reverse might be true: that the banishments had caused the fog. Admittedly, both these notions were controversial.

* * *

No, maybe I wasn't in the kitchen. Memories can deceive. I think I was asleep. Only when I woke did I discover that they'd escorted Revulo to the stony plains beyond the fires.

They hadn't let him collect his things, just a single change of clothes in a laundry sack. The ground was stony; the sun cracked his skin; the moon was cold. He lived on lichen and dew. At night he lay on the stones and held himself. He didn't sleep much. He'd wake to distant howlings, move on.

* * *

One morning he saw a single tree sticking up from the horizon. He walked all day to reach it. A curious tree: bare of leaves but full of animals. Small animals—cats, rabbits, squirrels—sat inches from each other in the upper branches. The trunk and the lower branches were crowded with wolves. Instead of bark, the tree appeared to have fur. The front of the pack scrabbled around and around in the fork of the tree. They kept starting to lunge at the animals higher up, then halting. It was clear that the higher branches might crack under their weight. They couldn't back up, either. More wolves had pushed up the trunk behind them. The animals in the upper branches sat motionless, trying not to catch attention, afraid of getting singled out and picked off—all except a small dog who twisted and turned round and round a branch, squirming higher and higher, trying, in defiance of all logic, to escape upwards.

Revulo stepped to the base of the tree. He opened his sack, not knowing what impelled him to do so. What happened next he has never been able to explain. Was it gravity? The force of a vacuum? The wolves drained into the sack in a long gray stream. He tied it closed, hoisted it onto his shoulder. It bulged and twisted. The weight made him list. He continued on, picking his way from stone to stone.

* * *

Sometimes the wolves squirmed so hard in the sack that they turned to mush. Then sometimes to liquid that went on churning until it volatilized. For a bit, his load would be lighter.

It was when the wolves were docile that they really weighed him down. Or when they slept. There were days when his legs wouldn't move. He lay curled around the sack, face in his hands, back turned to the sharp sun, the tickling wind. Afterwards he tried to forget those days.

* * *

At long intervals, he crossed paths with someone. Then at less long intervals. He began to encounter couples, small clans. Camps formed. Occasionally he approached to offer himself for odd jobs in exchange for a meal. Because of the wolves, he never spent the night.

* * *

I myself wandered; some men had requisitioned my house for training exercises. I wasn't forced to leave. They never noticed me, a childless old woman drifting through the rooms. But I noticed them.

As for the caravans of armored RVs and SUVs with tinted windows, we all skirted those. Revulo was especially careful. He ranged farther and farther afield, toward the horizon where the sun singed the curve of the earth. The fields of stone became fields of boulders. When he'd been safely alone for a couple days, he sometimes sat down and opened his sack. A gray blur would pour out, humping over the terrain, nosing and turning. When it found an unobstructed channel, it would accelerate, emulsify, resolve into galloping wolves.

* * *

Once, when he was very hungry and no one would give him work, I said, "I bet they'd listen to the wolves."

He looked at me for a long moment with his mouth open. Then turned his back and walked away.

* * *

There was nowhere to be alone in the camps. Sometimes I asked myself if I could walk out across the plains, like Revulo. I learned not to notice the smell of my body. After a few years, I heard that my house was empty. It took a couple more years to clear the weeds, repair the furniture, and paint over the stains on the walls. I moved slowly now. Evenings, I sat in bed and played video games. It was hard to imagine ever having cared about hamantaschen and popovers.

* * *

They say memory and imagination use the same part of the brain. My memories of Revulo began to feel like imagination. Intellectually, I knew he had existed—might still exist. Occasionally, travelers passed through town and claimed to have heard him on the plains. "Howling somewhere out of sight," they said. "Moaning in the middle of the night." Later, I heard a rumor that he had evaporated.

"You mean nobody in the camps has seen him," I said.

"No, literally," they said. "Any moisture out there, the sun completely sucks it up now."

Out there made me think of my binoculars. I found them in the basement and recovered my old habit of scanning the plains.

* * *

He'd thinned to a wisp and was hard to see. I spotted the bulging sack first.

"What if you released the wolves," I said, "away from any cities? I doubt people would recognize you. They need glaziers. You could easily have three meals a day."

"Ah. *If only I would* dot dot dot."

"Sorry," I said. "Bad habit of mine."

"Wait, why'd I have to say that, no, sorry, *I'm* sorry."

We sat down on a boulder. He opened his sack to show me: forty-eight stones, nothing but stones. He could put them down anywhere. Here, for instance. Except it was too late for him.

I resisted the impulse to argue. To say: you're just a cub, things can change, you have no idea, the changes since I was your age.

His face was as wrinkled as mine, his eyes brown shining moons. Wet with tears? I wasn't sure.

"You are—" I said. And stopped. No qualifiers. "You are."

"It's remarkable you can say that. I barely know you." Maybe I looked deflated, because he hesitated. "You have a vapor trail, is all I'm saying. Shadows, going back I'm not sure how far."

People who were gone before he was born. Moving inside me through brightly lit rooms.

"Top hats and parasols," he said with a smile.

I smiled back.

"Sorry, making a mess of this. I thought of you during some dark patches. *My stranger.* You didn't have to care. It meant a lot to me that you did. Saved my life, actually."

"And that means a lot to me," I said.

We grinned awkwardly at each other. His tears, if they were there, if I hadn't been misreading him, never fell. After a while, the wind picked up, blowing grit. He said, "you could go, now."

PETER GRANDBOIS

IN THE DREAM YOU WERE LARGE

We became trapped in the car on our fourth date. I was sure she was the one and had planned on asking her that night to mate for life. I know what you're thinking. Bats are promiscuous. They love to fool around. And I'll admit, I've used my sperm plug in the past to make sure whoever I was hot on didn't two-time me, but this was different. We'd waited. I even asked her if I could kiss her. Then one thing led to another and soon we were having sex in the back seat. I didn't know it could be like that. It was transcendent. I couldn't tell where I ended and she began. After, we fell asleep on the seat. That's when the humans must have arrived.

Don't rush to judgement. It was a cold October night on the north side of Chicago, and mating season was nearing an end. You can't blame us for seeking some shelter. I woke immediately and tried to shake Cecilia awake. I had no idea she'd be such a heavy sleeper. She peeled open one beautiful eye, and I pointed to the open rear window through which we'd entered. But just as I pulled her to an upright position several things happened simultaneously. In fact, it all happened so fast, and the events that followed were so traumatic, I'm not even sure of the order now or even of my part.

I'm pretty sure the rear doors opened on both sides. There were voices. Loud voices joking and laughing. There was only a moment to act. And my action, or lack of it, is the first of many things to haunt me from that night. I'd like to think I held on to her, grabbed her with my rear claw, and pulled her into the air in an attempt to fly past the bodies entering the car. I'd like to believe a stray elbow knocked her from my grasp, that I was not able to make it back to her, and so climbed the back seat just before the humans sat because I thought I'd caught a glimpse of her climbing as well. I'd like to think that when I saw the seat-belt hook on the ceiling of the car near the open window, I climbed toward it, not to escape but to gain a better vantage from which I could sound her location. Three people sat in that back seat. The driver closed the rear window, and I was left clutching the seat-belt hook. That's what I tell myself happened anyway. I wouldn't have simply abandoned her at the first sign of trouble. I couldn't have done that.

One of the passengers reached behind her to grab the seat belt. She didn't look behind her thankfully but rather pawed at the belt with her hand, grazing me with her fingers as she did so. "What a funny feeling seatbelt!" she exclaimed. "It's like big fuzzy dice." I held on tight with my rear claws and prayed she wouldn't turn around. After a few more paws, she found the belt and cinched it about her. That's when I heard Cecilia's muffled cries, as if she were calling me from deep underground. Those cries still haunt me. I hear them even now as I tell this tale for the thousandth time.

In my dreams I imagine myself hanging upside down, spreading my wings wide, and hissing wildly until the passengers turned around and fled in horror from the car. Sometimes I even see myself crawling across the car ceiling, then hanging there before their eyes, spreading my wings in all their glory. Then I rescue Cecilia from the seat where she's been trapped, pinned beneath the hindquarters of one of them. In my dreams, she's still okay. A little worse for the wear, but she's able to fly out the door the passengers left open when they ran screaming from the car.

The truth is, I hid, hanging upside down in the back from that seat belt hook, my wings folded around me, trying to block out Cecilia's cries, sounds outside the hearing range of humans, but unfortunately, not mine. Time flipped backwards and forwards, up and down, so that I have no idea how long we were in that car. Five minutes. Half an hour. An hour. Time, like so much of my life that night, lost all meaning. We stopped, and for a moment, as the passengers stepped out of the car, I had hope.

But then I saw her, sputtering and flapping on the seat, spinning in wounded circles. She let out another cry, this time in a lower frequency. "No!" I yelled. "Please, no! I'll get you out of here, but you've got to be quiet!" In her pain, she didn't or couldn't hear me. She cried out again, fluttering there in the middle of the seat. And that's when one of the passengers heard her cries. A woman. She turned around and screamed, pointing at Cecilia. "Oh my God!," she yelled. "I sat on a bat!" The others laughed at first, thinking she was joking. But then they heard Cecilia, too, and saw her flapping about the seat. "Jesus! Amy sat on a god-damned bat!" they said. In the confusion, I knew I had a brief moment in which to act. But no matter how hard I willed myself I didn't move. "Fly away, Cecilia!" I shouted." "Hurry, please! While you have time!" Of course, she couldn't do anything.

The one they called Amy grabbed a stick and knocked Cecilia from the seat. She landed on the pavement next to the car, where she continued her writhing. "What'll we do?" one of the humans asked. "We should put it out of its misery," Amy replied. "Good idea," the others agreed. The driver pulled his keys from his pocket and reached for the front door. "Stop!" I yelled and flew out into the night, shrieking at the lowest frequency

I could muster and flying as close to their faces as I could. At least that's the way I choose to remember it. They screamed and swatted at me, but I was too quick for them. I darted in and out, dive bombing them over and over until the driver said. "Listen guys, do you see that line. The haunted house is going to close soon, and we might not make it if we don't hurry. I vote we leave the bat. It'll be dead by the time we return." Though Amy hesitated, the rest murmured their assent, and, in the end, she went to stand in line with them. I was left alone with Cecilia.

Did I go to her? I'd like to believe I did. I'd like to think she died in my wings, as I held her close to me and sang our song. *O, my love. My darling. I hunger for your touch.* That's the way I remember it happening. It's what I tell myself happened. Whether I held her or not, I remember flying over that long line that led into the haunted house. I remember swooping down and grabbing at women's hair, clawing at men's faces, doing everything I could to scare them, to make them feel a fraction of the pain they'd caused me. And I remember, too, the vision of the haunted house rising before me. I remember how I caught sight of the shadow of a bat with red lights for eyes, bobbing up and down on a string in the second story window, as if mocking me. I remember thinking as I soared off into the light of the full moon, how nice to be like that bat, to have no memory of our part in this absurd world.

SAMARAH GREEVES

ODE TO A RENTAL PROPERTY

All you could ever want. Two windows and a door.
Enter the room with the harpsichord.
There's a blurred explosion of clover in the mirror.
Corded tassels cover the necks of bottles filled with Burgundy.
Ah (imagine a soothing sip), but all of this will be removed soon.
A plague on you, dear landlord.
And the bath, though tornado proof,
is no fortress against grotesque vesicles.

There is a lawn, which can be used for bowling.
But watch for the frogs, minuscule –
they can strike when you're not looking,
although they have never been a problem before.
There are no pillagers in this neighborhood,
but the skillet has been missing for some time now.

Call in the haruspex who doubles as this meadow's shepherd.
Sacrifice is a way of life with him.
But what about the orphans?
He tends to them and when they stop breathing
he carves spiracles with a scimitar
made from wooden ice cream spoons.

What about floods? No, never. Oh, maybe just a few drips.
After a hard rain. (Sure, I trust you.)

And whatever became of the past tenants?
Their separate tinctures, caught one below

the other as semi-glossy auras, are revealed
in the peeling layers of paint
close to the door and along the chair rail,
the paths of friction and hunger.

And the last one? He slides his chair back with a bark of insistence
taking one long last look before stepping into a sinkhole,
delightful with a bottomless well. (Cenote, they call them.) Cool, clear water.
It's Mayan, you know. Worth the sacrifice.

 CINDY VEACH

OOMANCY TRIGGERS
WITCH HUNT

Because albumen in water
    shape shifts

becomes bells, fingers, spires,
    becomes omen—

a future husband, his occupation
    but also, unexpectedly,

a *specter in the likeness of a coffin,*
    a *sign of diabolical molestation*—

Elizabeth & Abigail
    fell into fake fits

barking like dogs, complaining
    invisible spirits were pinching them—

therefore The Afflicted
    therefore The Accused.

Brooks, Rebecca, "Ann Putnam Jr: Villain or Victim?" 06 July 2015, History of Massachusetts Blog,
historyofmassachusetts.org/ann-putnam-jr/

 Jacob Bingham

TRAJECTORY

The story my aunt Peggy always tells my little cousins starts with a day when she was rocking on the porch in Papaw's rocking chair because he was gone with his brothers driving cattle three counties over. She always stops to tell the kids that Papaw walked the whole way, which Dad reminds me every time I complain about pretty much anything.

So with him gone so long, it was her job to sit on the porch and make sure nothing didn't go wrong.[1] A job that mostly involved listening inside to make sure my dad—she always points out he was just a tiny little thing back then—and his two friends weren't killing each other. She sat there in Papaw's rocking chair, listening and feeling her bare feet scrape when they pushed off the dusty porch she might need to sweep.

That's when she noticed how her feet seemed to make the porch and the house and the whole world grumble underneath her as she rocked forward and pushed off again. No, that wasn't her feet. She turned, knowing what she would find. It wasn't in their driveway. Not the creek neither. Not the hill after that nor in the road—Praise God. But somewhere in the hill on the other side of the road. On its way down from The Flat.[2] Something bent each tree gently back as it stepped closer to the edge of the forest. She couldn't see the giant yet.

It's hard to keep a screen door from slamming against the frame a few times, but she managed despite her rush to get back inside. The sound of thumping boy feet moved all over the house while my dad and his two childhood friends chased each other.

Gerald saw my aunt enter and ran to her holding his knobby, homemade slingshot. "Peggy, Roger ain't playing right."

She crouched behind the green couch next to the window and said, "You hush your mouth!"

Gerald covered his mouth and widened his eyes at my aunt. "Don't you witch me, Peggy. I swear I'll tell your daddy if you go casting some witch spell on me."

---

1   This is when you would expect someone to ask "Where was Mamaw?" or "You ain't even the oldest sister. Why was you in charge?" But if someone tried, she would have just said something like, "Yuns hush and let me tell it."

2   The Flat is what my family calls the top of the mountain where Dad farms and where they bury people. It's not flat at all.

She put her index finger to the floor and started drawing shapes in the dust. "Boy, if you don't shut your mouth and lay down on this floor, I'll witch you so that you can't never tell nobody nothing."

The house started shaking. Big shakes with sets of little ones between, and she saw in a vision—like from God—that giant's smooth feet crushing everything without getting a scratch or even a mark on them. Closer to the house. Roger and Dad's dirty little feet too, pattering across the sloping wood floors on their way to the living room.

Gerald must not have seen any vision from God because when he felt all that shaking he cried and said, "No, Peggy. Please don't witch me. I'm sorry. I won't never talk again in my whole damned[3] life I swear."

"If you're gonna use language like that, then you may as well keep your mouth shut. The Lord didn't give you a mouth so you could cuss all over his creation."

Dad and Roger stomped into the room, panting and saying, "Peggy, what the hell is that?" Then they kept running, but this time around Peggy and Gerald, until Roger saw something out the window. He stopped so fast Dad didn't have time to react and he collided with the back of Roger's head. When they fell between Peggy and Gerald, Dad's face bounced off the back of Roger's head with a crunch and an arc of blood. He scrambled to his feet, wailing.

Peggy just kept saying, "No, no, hush, no, Russell, hush."

And Gerald was saying something like, "See, now I told you Roger wasn't doing right. Didn't I tell you? Peggy, just send Roger's big ass up the path if he ain't going to play right. You want me to do it for you? I can."

Dad was standing there with his hands covering his nose and mouth. He had hushed. Red peeked out from the opening between the bottom of his hands and twisted down his forearm. He dropped his hands to his sides and revealed his blood-covered palms. Peggy always tells the kids he looked like the Lord except younger. She doesn't mention that Dad's skin was probably lighter too. Dad stared past the living room and through the plastic insulation that clouded his parents' single pane windows. "Shit, Peggy. I believe they's a giant coming out there," he said, blood popping off his lips.

"I know, dummy. I been telling ya'll to hush." She was still on the floor, waving her hands for the boys to just please get down.

---

3   It takes some begging and the assistance of a few older cousins saying "Come on, Peggy," but you can get the more accurate version of Gerald and Roger's dialogue out of my aunt when the grandchildren aren't around.

Gerald said, "Well, son of a bitch, Peggy. You could have told me that shit a long time ago and I would have just hushed my mouth right there. You didn't have to go acting like you was about to send me to Hell with some witch curse."

Roger kicked Gerald in the shin. "You better shut your damn mouth or I'll tell mom and she'll cut your little wrinkly pecker off."

Through the window, they saw a fuzzy image of a human figure at least as tall as a barn. It had stopped now and was turning to face the house.

It spoke in a whispered shout. "I smell your blood. You come out and I leave everyone else alone. No reason to act uncivilized over one snack."

They all looked at Dad, but this part of the story always changes. Sometimes Russell Bingham puts up a fight, says it has to be one of the other boys on account of he's the last of his line. That's a law. Sometimes he is on his way out before they can shout for him to stop. Sometimes no one speaks. He starts to cry and wipes enough blood off his face to appear in control. Maybe he tells Peggy he loves her. Maybe he tells Roger and Gerald to split his toy cars. In one version, Peggy tries to stop him but the other boys somehow manage to hold her down. In another, she says, "I figured Mommy and Daddy could just make another boy, and maybe they'd even do better next time."

One way or another, he walks out onto the front porch and the screen door bounces in the frame twice before closing.

* * *

Then Peggy always stops her story to ask Dad what he said since she wasn't out there.

Dad says, usually with his mouth half full, that he walked right out onto the porch and that big old giant was just standing butt naked out in the gravel driveway. The kids either laugh or pretend this is gross. Dad waits and chews his ham before he tells them giants are too big. They can't get clothes from nowhere. Next, Dad says the giant waved his hand like he wanted Dad to come on, but Dad told him he may as well to just go away because nobody here wasn't worth eating no way. If he wanted a nice pig or a hen or something they could give him one of those, but the Binghams was too scrawny for eating.

Dad's version ends when the giant says he reckoned he'd just have him one of them pigs then. But the kids are never satisfied with this ending. They look at Peggy who says Dad was probably the one who ate the pig. Then she goes back to her story.

* * *

Peggy snatched the slingshot from Gerald and ran out the backdoor. She jumped off the back porch and ran down the gravel driveway that wrapped around to the front of the house. Along the way, she picked up a handful of stones and—wouldn't you know it—there were five of them. [4]

Peggy checked her five stones. One was an arrowhead, and she knew Dad would probably want it for his collection. When Peggy came around the corner of the house, she saw the giant on one knee and reaching toward Dad. The giant must have heard Peggy then because he turned his head to her. She dropped the other four stones for the arrowhead and saw that it had already cut her. It was heavy and the tip was sharp like God had shaped it for her that day out of his wrath and mercy. She loaded it into the slingshot and pulled back, feeling the eager arrowhead pressing itself forward to meet its foe.

Dad stepped off the front porch, yelling something, and pointing toward the barn. The giant's silk hair whipped in the same direction Dad pointed. The wind started blowing so hard it pulled Peggy toward the giant. She claims old people said giants could bring their own weather, but she knows that wind was from God.

Peggy whispered that the battle was the Lord's and the wind delivered her message right to the giant's ear[5] just before she released the arrowhead and let God's own winds take it too. Her aim was horrible. The arrowhead was going to hit his bellybutton at best and with so little force that the giant might think she missed completely, but the battle was the Lord's. The arrowhead curved upward in the wind and even started to spiral so that—when it reached its appointed place—the point drilled deep into the giant's forehead. Still on one knee, his torso slumped forward toward Dad and the porch, but he rolled over as he fell, ending up on his back in front of the house.

Dad's friends came running outside talking about how Peggy must have witched that stone and killed the son of a bitch. Dad walked over to Peggy and asked if that was an arrowhead she used to kill it.

When Papaw came home, he found a bunch of barefoot kids staring at a barefoot giant corpse that was cleaner than any of them had been in weeks. He had doused it in gasoline and was just about to burn it when Mamaw told him he'd better not. She crawled onto the giant's head and stuck her hand into the hole in his forehead. Peggy claims blood rolled up from the hole and over her hand when she yanked the bloodstained arrowhead out. Red painted tiny rivers in the wrinkles between the giant's eyebrows[6]. After she waved

---

4   1 Samuel 17:40

5   Don't ask me how she knows what he heard.

6   When you're a kid you don't think to ask if blood could still flow like that from a dead giant. Now, I don't see the point in questioning the blood thing if I'm going to accept the giant and Papaw's magic.

her hand and walked away, Papaw swiped his thumb three times on the flap of his overalls and held it up in front of the corpse. He blew just over his thumb as if it was a candle and the giant ignited.[7]

*   *   *

I don't usually make it to my aunt Peggy's Christmas party anymore, but that doesn't excuse me from her stories. Wherever I am on Christmas Eve, no matter how long I stay awake praying or talking to my wife or burning out my only eye with the white light of my phone, I eventually dream about Peggy's giant.

It starts like any dream: I'm naked. Except this time I'm walking through a forest. The trees bend away on each side, blown by a gentle breeze that spreads out from me in every direction. The trees don't crack or splinter and the wind isn't even strong enough to be pushing them; they're just giving me space. Or maybe huddling together to ask if anyone has ever seen me before.

Then I'm walking in the woods, and I look down just in time to see my foot land on a mound of translucent, eggs? They pop under my feet and deer ticks swarm over my skin that I now notice was so clean before. Only some of the ticks are fat although I can't say what they got fat on if they never left the nest. The layers of ticks shift and crawl and I start running to find some water I can jump into, but I don't run. You know how your body almost never listens to you in a dream. As hard as I try, I'm still just walking and looking at my feet. The itching I expect never comes as the crawling mass loses interest in me, thins, disappears under leaves. I'm clean again and still walking.

When I look up, it's not even woods anymore. It's the road my grandparents used to live on. This part changes. If I remember that I've had this dream before, I want to go left, but these clean feet don't let me. If I remember trying to go left and failing, I go right with the intent of walking past Papaw's and on to my parents' house.

But it doesn't matter. Every time, these clean feet take me right down the road and then they turn left into Papaw's driveway that wraps around his house, and I hear someone whistling. It sounds like it's coming from behind me, so I turn to look. The whistling gets louder and sounds like it's flying out of the woods right toward me until it lands in my mouth. Until it's me, whistling and walking with these clean feet down their driveway.

---

[7]   It would be rude to ask where Mamaw was this whole time, so I don't. Am I supposed to believe both parents decided to leave their kids to watch themselves while they walked three counties over to sell cattle? Or was she there the whole time and she somehow didn't notice this giant's loud footsteps or the sound of screaming, cursing, bloody children who couldn't have been more than two rooms away. I've been in that house. You can hear someone scratch their head from the opposite end.

The sound of a screen door bouncing against the frame comes from the porch that I know is on the other side of the house. I try to dig my heels into the gravel, but the wind comes in from behind me now. It slides me forward, leaving trails in the gravel. It whips strands of silk hair into my eyes—I have two in the dream—and my mouth. I don't taste anything.

Standing in front of the porch, I forget how this dream ends. I'm at Papaw's and when was the last time I saw him? He has four stone steps that take me, willingly, up to his green porch. Past the rocking chair he always sat in to watch the dogs.

Still whistling, I knock on the door frame. I want to say, "Papaw, are you home? It's Little Walter."

But I hear lots of shushing coming from inside, and my mouth says, "You kids all right in there? Somebody hurt?"

It never seems strange to me that I smell a broken nose through the screen door. A smell so thick I can taste it. Something feels like it's crawling in my stomach. I can't remember eating.

My mouth starts again. "Come on, now. Maybe there's some way I can help."

A drop of blood hits the floor inside and the smell splashes through the whole hollow. It's not long before Dad is at the door, but he's just a kid with a smashed nose that folds to the left. A trail of blood has run down from it and covered his mouth. It sits in streaks like thin cuts along his shirt.

He pushes the screen door open and steps on to the porch. His bare feet point at mine, and his look like my feet should. Mine just look clean and smooth and too long. Not to mention my feet meet bare legs leading up to bare everything else.

When it sinks in that I'm naked, Dad's eyebrows draw together and he makes sure his eyes stay on my face. "Where the Hell is your clothes?" He points to Papaw's barn, trying to keep an eye on me without really looking at me. The blood on his hand is already starting to dry. "You may as well get on to the barn and have you a hen or a nice pig or something. Ain't nobody in here worth eating no way. Too scrawny."

The hen is too small to be of any interest. The pig though. I can imagine his squealing, his bones and hooves popping under the pressure of my teeth. Even if I can't imagine how I'd even fit an entire pig in my mouth or how I'd think about eating such a disgusting animal. The kids, at least, would probably be a little cleaner.

I hear the feet pattering up the stone steps behind me, but I'm watching Dad as long as I can. He looks like me except younger and bloody. When I hear the slingshot tighten back there on the steps, it cuts me off before I can ask Dad if he knows me.

This body turns on its own to see Peggy with wrath-of-God eyes like my sister's except without her fire and brimstone hair. She has the slingshot pulled back and an arrowhead loaded between two fingers so it points toward me. The four rocks she knows she doesn't need rattle down the porch steps.

I put my hands up and the wind howls through the porch so that I can only half see through the veil of black hair streaming over my face. Half-squatting to appear smaller, I say, "Whoa, now. I just wanted a snack. If that's too much to ask, I'll be on my way." For once, I agree with most of what my body decides to say.

Peggy closes one eye and says, "Hush your mouth, glutton."

The wind stops long enough for me to hear the little feet landing on the threshold behind me. I should know who they are, but their names haven't caught up to their feet yet. When the wind returns it has chosen a direction: it blows from behind Peggy, sending the arrowhead whistling straight for me. It doesn't hit my forehead like it should. Down and to my right. The point bursts my eyeball and digs its way inside. Now I'm only seeing out of the left like usual.

The names catch up to the little feet and I know Dad is back there with his friends, Gerald and Roger, and they are all holding their pocketknives. Their little hands slither around my hair and onto my shoulders as they pull me back. I twitch with each bite from the pocketknives and every time I want to ask don't they know me. But Dad hasn't even made me yet, and I'm stuck inside some traveler. They keep biting, cottonmouths who won't stop until the prey quits twitching.

* * *

Or maybe Papaw and his five remaining brothers at least rode horses three counties over instead of walking. Of course they would. Maybe Peggy rocked on the porch and thought about school on Monday. About who has to feed when her daddy drives cattle. About ringing a chicken's neck or not sticking a pig or when her little brother will be old enough to do that old nasty shit himself. And about how she shouldn't say shit, so was it really different to think it?

Then she heard whistling on the road that curved around the hill surrounding their hollow. Somewhere between her and the gently swaying trees. The whistle grew louder.

It's hard to keep a screen door from bouncing against the frame a few times, so she didn't bother. It bounced. The sound of Dad and his two friends, Roger and Gerald, screamed through the house.

Gerald heard her come in, and I've heard the story so many times the same way that he must have run in with his knobby, homemade slingshot and said, "Peggy, Roger's big ass ain't playing right."

But I bet she just got down on the floor and said, "Hush, Gerald. They's somebody out there."

And Gerald shouted, "I ain't laying down in no damn floor with you, woman. My daddy taught me better than that. He said a woman will take every nickel a man has if he lays down with her just one good time."

"Gerald. You ain't got no danged nickels. Now will you get away from that window and hush?"

The wind that had gently blown the trees before became a storm, like it always does in Kentucky, and flashes lit the house through the plastic insulated windows. The walls growled as if to ward away trespassers.

Gerald somehow ended up on the floor next to my aunt. "Peggy, if you was just scared of the storm, you could of said so."

Dad ran into the room and pointed to his sister and his friend on the floor. "Ew, Peggy. What the hell?"

Roger came slapping his bare feet on the floor just as Dad turned away from Peggy. When Roger couldn't stop in time, his forehead collided with Dad's nose. The thunder masked the sound of bone cracking. They fell to their butts and stared, linked in tragedy. Roger's face changed first when he saw Dad's zig-zag nose and the silken blood sliding over his lips.

Roger, with his hand on his forehead, said he was sorry, which brought Dad to wailing tears. Gasps as spit mixed with blood and formed red bubbles over his open mouth.

Peggy just kept saying, "No, no, hush, no Russell, hush."

And Gerald reminded Peggy that Roger's big ass wasn't playing right and sending him up the path was probably the best option.

They all hushed when they realized someone was whistling outside the door. The information of the last few minutes came back to them and stacked onto the present: the sound of boots on the porch steps, the knocking on the door, more wind, more thunder.

A voice that said, "Hey. You kids all right in there? Somebody hurt?"

No one had to beg for silence now. They all kept quiet as if he would tell himself he was just hearing things.

"Come on, now. Isn't there something a man can do for you?"

Dad stared at his blood, dripping and spreading on the floor. Dragging down along the slope.

This part of the story always changes because my family needs it to. Peggy grabbed Gerald's slingshot and told Dad to answer the danged door. She took the back door and grabbed some wet stones from the gravel driveway curving around the house. Dad stood on the front porch saying something about his mommy being out at the barn. Peggy grabbed the arrowhead from the five stones and loaded it into the slingshot, accidentally dropping the other stones in the process.

She stood drenched behind the man whose hat nearly scraped the porch roof. He turned at the sound of the stones clattering on the porch. One hand left his hat and the other came up. Surrender. The storm ripped the hat from his head and shreds of his silk hair whipped around his face.

He half-squatted to appear smaller. "Whoa, now. I just came for a snack. If that's too much, I'll be on my way."

Peggy closed one eye. "You hush. I know you're one of them giants. You all should of stayed up north. Ate them people up there."

"A giant? Honey, where are your parents? Someone needs to look at your brother's nose here." The man rested on one knee and brought his hands down.

She glanced at the barn. "Glutton. I said shut your mouth."

"For the love of God, kid." He twisted to see Gerald and Roger creeping up to join Dad behind him, then he turned back to Peggy as he started to stand. "Look. I don't know what you think you're going to do with a slingshot anyway. "

And she let it go. The point of the arrowhead hit his right eye. It made him flinch and maybe reach for his face, but there's no way it killed him. Peggy told Dad to get him, and the man probably thought he had fallen into a copperhead den as Dad and his friends jabbed at his shoulders and neck with their pocketknives. They pulled him down and jabbed until he stopped twitching while Peggy watched. She thought about saying Stop. That's too much. You'll kill him.

But you can't feel sorry for the fox if you want to keep your chickens.

They heard, "Lord, children. What's this?" Mamaw stood on the porch steps. The white plastic aura of her rain poncho covered her so only her long nose was wet. She held a hen in her elbow, its head sagging forever from its broken neck.

The boys, armed and bloody, said, "We had to. We had to."

Peggy said, "Mommy, he was a giant come to eat Russell. There wasn't nothing else we could do."

"Lord God, Peggy. What have yuns done?" Mamaw dropped the hen on the porch. She took the man's hands and began to drag him into the yard. "I reckon he is pretty big."

While they watched her take him to the woodpile, Dad picked up the arrowhead, now red with giant's blood, and stuck it in his pocket. When Mamaw came back, the man's body sprawled alone beside the woodpile.

She told Peggy, "When that rain quits, you burn him. We don't want no more of them come looking for him, you hear?" But she knew the rain wouldn't stop until Peggy had already gone to bed, so she'd be the one shuffling outside in the dark to start a fire.

She saw her son's crooked nose, his swollen eyes, and the dry blood covering his mouth. After removing her plastic rain poncho and retrieving the dead hen, she took Dad's hand and led him back into the house. "Did that man do that to your nose, Russell?"

Gerald followed her in and said, "Wasn't no giant did that, Pearl. It was Roger's big ass. He ain't played right all day."

 JENNY GRASSL

TWO POEMS

WHITENESS AND THE ALCHEMISTS

had I understood what I held in my hands
one thousand white cranes   flown as steam
from the flowers condensed on surface sloe
and all midnight   cooked in the subliming pot
shadows peeled from our white bodies
brewed in an old water with long stems of tulips
fermented   had I held onto   one vial
of chaos   a measure of black earth   and rested
in the hour of the wolf   had those on the far side
of the world   not wished   as we did   to make
a potion for life   with pale stir of sulfur
and saltpeter   cooked with charcoal   had they
not   changed the odds   with this unintended
gunpowder   had the fire arrows never flown
and lit the sky   all the dark bodies now distilled
into statistic   death in this bright alembic
had I myself not burned Nigredo   looking
for Albedo   how did it get to be about precious
metal   black   whitening

SHE   SLIPPING INTO EARTH SKIN

snow drives alive as a body meant for death
for dream   cancels day   it is evening
it is over   the criss cross of crows
closes the field she chooses   the dark
marks her   a hesitation of tracks
then a halt to behold   the new penny sun's
slant-split crackle of old solidago and sedge tops
final acts of briar rose against the snow
coyotes howling at her back   she runs across dusk
husk of the field's thinnest pink   as the sun sets
a half corona flames along a mountain back
will the granite heart of it beat   as the earth sets
with no pine or bobcat   no light to limn a-linger
a world of dynamic rock will rule unto granule
until ground down by diamonds of its greed
a last spinning beauty   just the powdered
roundness of earth   a grinding of its teeth
she enters house and sleep in the cold phone
bedside   of time   slattern of the dream dome
she strays   forest frondle   moss sparks
and honey fungus spring from the dead   wood
until dawn the room peels from   a wallpaper
she steps out of   in dried glue and pheromones
floral   she stands naked next to a crack in the wall
that follows her curve   two caryatids
keeping winter off their heads   though it blows
through dream-pocked ruin of her   on a planet
porous like pumice   the mares of night tire
and turn to home and curry comb   it is December
leaving her half-slept with a half moon in blue
flipping like a fish on a dock

STACEY LEVINE

WHERE IS MICE?
An Excerpt

The novel *Where Is Mice?* takes place in a Miami neighborhood during the Cold War. There, the book's narrator, Girtle, and a teen girl with the unfortunate nickname "Mice," get acquainted with their new neighborhood.

I moved through high, breezeblown grass past elderberry shrubs, looking for Mice. I climbed between slats in the wooden fence. From that vantage point, I saw The Blur for the first time.

He was a small, thin man dressed in recluse-brown; I knew from weeks of listening to neighbors that he'd lived on Reef Way all his life. The Blur, whose given name was unknown to me until that day, routinely roamed, in white gym shoes, the boulevard and all the neighborhood's splinter streets, alleyways, unidentified paths, and trails, too; and while residents sometimes joshed The Blur—merely to distract him from his troubles, they always said—they also spoke heavily among themselves about The Blur's skin, which was spotted with common acne. They often mentioned knowingly, too, that The Blur was contradictorily arrogant to some extent despite being shy. The Blur lived in someone's basement.

But while the usually sweaty and worked-up Blur was unquestionably part of Reef Way, always invited, even if provisionally, to social occasions, Mice, I compared in my mind, remained outside of everything.

The Blur sprinted past me through the dusty alley so smoothly and silently that I thought he was a thrown ball or low hawk, and nearing Mice, who crouched in the alley beside Parrotts Grocery, he pointed at her, hollering geyserlike into her face, "AHAHAAHA!"

From a certain point of view, his abrupt noise-spouting was understandable, since anyone laying eyes on Mice for the first time tended to startle at her smallness and heavy head of white hair. The sun-woozy neighbors on the porch looked over the railing as The Blur and the girl, both competitors for some bottommost rank in the neighborhood, eyed each other. Then The Blur began speaking slowly, sea-wave style, glancing up intermittently at the porch-sitting neighbors, his words tossing and catching on his breath's crests as he addressed Mice: "Everyone knows *me*. But what are *you*?"

The girl rebutted instantly, "What are *you*?"

Neighbors laughed in their chairs.

No doubt Mice had learned to deliver phrases in sharp tones from her sister and, in general, the siblings' longstanding practice of making stakes of words: poles and demarcations.

With her compromised eyesight, Mice appeared to struggle seeing The Blur and edged closer to him; The Blur backed away. From the porch, behind a post, Twing wiped his face, coughing a few times as if to say: There's a substantial difference between us up here and you down there.

As cicadas' chirrups crescendoed high in the trees, Twing leaned back slowly in his sun-warmed chair and seemed to fall asleep, the newspaper floating against his face and scraping his beard's stiff hairs, settling there.

In the alley, The Blur asked the girl, "Are you aware that life is temporary?"

"Yes I am. But I don't mind."

Sometimes I envied Mice's freedom from guile.

"How do you fill your days?" continued the outcast-looking Blur with his messy hair to Mice.

"With radios."

Neighbors on the porch chuckled at this, though Mice and The Blur drew closer as if instinctively, forming a type of cloche between them and exchanging quieter words, excluding the porch-sitters, who continued listening nevertheless.

"*My* days aren't empty. I've always lots of laundry to do," said The Blur softly, his thick saliva putting corners around his words, shortening them. "I wish I had a hobby. I own flasks so I could try some chemistry experiments but I never have."

"I like wire," said the girl.

The bank's security guard Ron Brahms stepped forward, arms crossed. "If you want to do chemistry experiments just do them."

"Well I'm a little afraid to—on my own," The Blur answered, squinting at Brahms.

Old Twing was awake suddenly, flailing with the newspaper, calling over the railing: "Was the first chemist in the world afraid? By god no. He jumped into his experiments right away. And that's what you should do Fred. Stop lollying and live your life!"

So Fred is The Blur's name, I told myself.

He ignored Twing and continued to Mice sheepishly, "The truth is I've wasted about every day of my life. I played checkers for a decade but that's not productive. I couldn't stop playing. But everything changed just a few weeks ago."

"Why?" the girl asked.

"Well I'm not sure but everything's different now. I'm extremely busy and I'm studying for a big test."

Neighbors on the porch, scooting their chairs closer to the railing, listenened to this, all eyes on Mice and The Blur, who finished: "When I was a senior at Slaughter High you see I stopped going to catch-up algebra and I failed."

"Fred I thought you graduated!" cried old Phenice from the porch.

This seemed to incite a form of rage in The Blur, who turned to holler at the elder, "I *did not* graduate! I never passed algebra because on exam day my foot got caught on the staircase railing and—"

"Oh that was *so long* ago Fred," stressed Brahms, rolling his thumbs as two miniature logs. "Nineteen-twenny years? You can't retake that test *now*."

"Why not take it? Take it!" said Parrott.

"Oh I *will* take it," The Blur exhorted at the small grocer, his face suddenly running with tears. "I'll hate every second of that test! But I'll take it. It'll finally be over."

"Say. I know what year you *should*'ve graduated Fred," Cissy drawled, pushing and wiggling her elbow's loose skin, then her hand moved to play daintily at her hair. "It was nineteen—"

The Blur plugged his ears with his fingers, exploding, "Don't say the name of the year! Don't!"

Here, neighbors broke out in a hearty round of laughter.

"It was a bad-luck year," the awkward man tried explaining, and Parrott shook his head impatiently as if the unappealing Blur were beyond repair.

The Blur turned to him. "Miss Kidd said I could take the test during the kids' summer school! I'm scheduled to retake it next month. Don't you dare say I won't pass it!"

"I'm not saying anything," the grocer answered indifferently.

Studying The Blur carefully from my hidden position in the fence, I realized he was not a boy, but a man, and his face—less-so his eyes—was vastly smoother and younger than he was. Then The Blur shook his head at the failings which seemed to weigh ponderously on him and which he had yet to overcome. "Aunt said if I pass the test next week then I can graduate."

"Graduate from high school now?" said Twing, finally understanding, yet puzzled. "Twenty years later?"

The Blur sweated. "I should be studying *now*! I barely have time though."

"Y'mean y'barely have brains?" laughed Brahms, glancing at the others.

The Blur cried at this jab, then hiccupped. "Stop it!"

"You get off yer duff an' do something with yer life before it ends!" Twing called roughly over the newspaper's edge.

They laughed more, but Cissy cut them off crossly. "Twing said something true: Life ends. Actually it doesn't *go* fast but it *ends* fast."

Twing ignored her. "An' don't get any plumper Fred or they won't letcha take th'test," he added in a cough-laced voice. "Because...y'know know the old saying—'Whale rhymes with jail.'"

"That's not a *saying*!" the Blur, purplish, screamed at him; then he looked at Brahms. "See the reason I can't study is because the moment we're born we start to die—so Cissy's right. Death is too distracting! Still...I'll try studying the book five minutes each day. Then I'll progress—won't I?"

"Nope," said Brahms, heavily comfortable in his chair.

The Blur wept in one running breath, looking to and fro at the porch-sitters while sweat-soaked at this point even through the rubber waist of his gym pants: "I may pass yet! I bought a red pencil for studying!" He withdrew a stubby pencil from a pocket, holding it high in the air.

Neighbors began to lose interest and reclined back into their chairs, Cissy commenting, eyes closing in the sun, "Who'll grade your algebra test Fred twenty years after the fact? Miss Kidd won't—she teaches Kindergarten."

"Someone *will*!" The Blur screamed angrily, tearily, everything at stake.

"Lotsa people blubber when they talk about their old schools," Hildy nodded. "Oh I've seen it many times."

"Why do they blubber I wonder?" Phenice asked her.

"Oh that's easy," said a home nurse who had just joined them on the porch, sitting beside old Phenice, taking the old woman's pulse with two fingers while submerging the thumb of the same hand into a cup presumably containing liquid, as if the home nurse was either soaking the thumb or gauging the liquid's temperature. "They cry because of all the time that's passed and because they'll die someday soon."

"Maybe that's *not* the reason," posited Cissy.

"It *is*," stressed the home nurse. "People always cry when things change. That's how they are."

Twing yawned wide, slumping once more behind the paper; I never saw him again.

Out of the corner of my eye, I finally spied Mice and was relieved, for it was my responsibility to keep her in sight. She was dashing across the far end of the alley toward a heavy apple tree; I sprang after her weightlessly, tearing past the elderberry shrubs and their jagged-edged leaves so horribly similar to hemlock leaves and their toothy edges. I tensed: which plant was which? I vowed to sidestep all plants and their roots. Then I remembered that the elderberry's fruit is not poisonous, though the branches are, so I relaxed somewhat.

 KYLE ROWLAND

BESTIARY

In loving memory of Grandpa Bob Rowland.
Save us a seat in the ice cream shop just up the road.

You feared the trees and the demons they harbored,
with their dead bear faces, performing arachnid gymnastics,
haunting the canopies of climbable crabapple and spruce.
You never knew what magic they used to remain unseen,
if the ambling possum was their thrall, the steller's jay their spy.
They lingered like Willamette mist, formless, yet present,
claiming young meals of the careless and wild variety,
each case cold without a trace, he said,
except for a single shoe left behind
that was just about your size, or a plastic bike helmet
the same sun-faded purple as your own.

The only word you had then was *grandfather*,
but he was a shotgun augur,
demystifier of ratty fishing line,
a sockeye and steelhead-savvy haruspex
telling you of three-toed cryptids carousing in cornfields
with crow-bone moonlight men of ancient origins who,
right after you went to bed,
thieved toys and trading cards, stashing them away in little pocket universes.
And he knew all too well the terrible powers of Peruvian mummies
who could peel themselves off the pages of National Geographic
to torment you in the backseat, on his command, if you continued to complain.

Ghoulfish

Untitled #4

Untitled #7

 KATIE QUARLES

PROZAC

In the middle of me is a crater. The doctor says it can't be filled. All can be done is rub and pat the sides with mud so it won't crumble further. Me and the moon are besties. It's become a bowl of blueberries. My mother paints my face with crushed moon. I'm in a plastic wedding gown, bound, about to be executed. "We need to love like we used to." It's my last statement. I'm red-faced and grateful. Mother's not ready for me to be nothing, but nothing's a something I'm used to leaning my hands against. The blueberries form a thumb that's up, but the claqueurs' timing's hell-bent.

 CYNTHIA ZHANG

MARIA PETRANOV

Eleven months into the marriage, they eat Maria Petranov.

They joke about it, at the ceremony, about how her husband will be impatient and she will not last a month—the boy so young after all, barely out of college, of course he will not be able to wait—but in the end, it takes him eight months longer than his brother, eleven months and two weeks to the day. Almost three times the normal rate, and that is close, that is dangerous, that is the exact kind of situation such marriages between the New and Old Peoples were supposed to prevent. *Too young,* they will whisper, just out of Stanford and barely more than a child, what were they thinking, putting him to it?

But they do not know that now. In the moment, sitting in light oak pews as bride and groom walk up the aisle, there is none of that danger, no portent of future fear, only this: the pale petals drifting through the air, the white of her dress against the black of his suit, diamond on her hand and flower around his wrist.

It is a good ceremony. When the minister places their hands together, joining them, he hesitates a moment before leaning forward to kiss her, and they laugh at that, indulgent with wine and the presence of new love. *Lovely,* the guests—his guests—murmur, New People draped in velvet and silk, their eyes jewel-bright and skin the color of marble. She ought to appreciate it, while it lasts.

Her family, small and grey as Maria Petranov herself, watch with wide, hungry eyes. Dressed in stiff black and dusty shoes, they do not cheer, do not smile.

There had been no volunteers that year, no young bride willing to offer herself up for the good of her people, and so it had come back to the old agreements: blood ties and the rotating list of old contracted families, descendants of the nobles who had agreed to serve the Princess Eva and her lover so long ago. And so, this; and so, her, Maria Petranov, the beginnings of crow's feet and calloused fingers, over a decade older than her husband and the start of grey in her hair. No innocent dewy maiden, too much time out in the world and away, but untainted all the same. Untouched, and thus suitable.

In the aftermath, at the reception, they crowd her—aunts and uncles, in-laws of in-laws and far-off grandparents, the New People come to inspect their new prize. *Pretty pretty,* they croon, but she is not pretty—too old for that and too thin, bones sticking out like grotesque jewelry. Perhaps she had once been beautiful, the long line of her neck and arc of her nose hinting at former grace, but there is none of that now in her sallow skin, her cracked and pale lips. But that is alright, that is fine; that is what the ceremony is for, after all.

Behind them, her relatives stand, faces stone-still as they watch.

You will be such a treat, the New People whisper, leaning forward, fingers tracing sharp cheekbones, tugging at hair the color of old blood and ashes, *such a beautiful beautiful treat.*

The words are not friendly, far less kind, but Maria Petranov does not only flinch, only gazes back with dark, impassive eyes.

And then she smiles.

She smiles at them, with her old woman's mouth and burnt coal eyes, and there is something ancient about her in that moment, older than the stars and wiser than the gods—something ancient, and so gently amused.

They move into the house a week after the wedding.

Perched over a steep drop of cliff on the outskirts of town, the house is a familiar sight: the same house others have used year after year, possibly the same one where Eva and Isen first made their pact, the pale human princess and that first silent stone knight joining their peoples with a kiss—but even they, New People who hold their history against their skin, cannot remember. It could be, for all they know. It certainly looks the part, jagged stone cornices circling up the roof and frozen gargoyles perched in the eaves like images imported from some dusty folk story. A maid comes around beforehand, but the scent of age stays—a faded, musty odor, older than mothballs and dust, pervasive in the walls themselves. It is there in the air itself, the softness of the leather, the patterns carved into the headboards and the worn wood of the dressers. An ancientness to it all: to eat there, at this same table where generations sat before, sleep in the same bed where strings of couples slept before, hundreds of bodies writhed and joined together in ceremony old as the ground below their feet. The same house where, when it is time, it will happen: the final wedding rites consummated, blood spilt on stone and bringing new life to them all.

It is not an inviting building; but as they stand there, gazing at the house looming before them, he takes her hand—hesitant, a little afraid—and she smiles at him and is, for a moment, almost beautiful.

When everything has passed, empty bottles of champagne cleared away and all the guests gone at last, it is only this which remains: two figures, hands gripped and standing together against the dark.

The honeymoon does not last long. A few days, and they are already back to routine. He goes back to work, suit rumpled, tie strangling his neck and business cards in one hand. She stays inside, no use in continuing to returning to her job—lawyer or doctor or newly appointed professor, something terribly unseemly like that, but then again, she was older than ordinary and allowances must be made—when she could not stay. Besides, she has new duties now: lines of statues waiting to be dusted in the foyer, tea to be poured for the contingent of New guests and well-wishers, dead garden beds to prepare for the changing of the seasons. Time to rest and eat, grow soft and sweet for their coming feast.

And yet—

Yet for all that, the fine skein of normalcy, there is something off. She sits there, dusting the old furniture, smiling at the parade of visitors, second cousins and great-aunts come with casseroles and congratulations, smiles pyrite bright; he goes to work, attends the dinner parties and soirees, smiling at the right times and shaking hands with the right people, but it is not the same. It is the way he stands, dressed in his pressed tuxedo and new shoes—the line of his stance, the twist of his face. Some cadence in the way he speaks, mouth smiling but eyes always distant. As though he is not there but somewhere far away.

Love, the older women guess, and shake their heads at it, smiling.

And indeed there is something sweet about it, something that engenders such indulgence. His face when he looks at her sometimes, a sideways half-smile on his lips as if perpetually astonished she is still there. T   he tenderness with which he holds her hands, as if afraid she will disappear, dissolve like a dream-woman inside a summer daydream. Love in such marriages is not unheard of, but it is rare, and the gossip-mongers circle it, drawn by the novelty. *Sentimental,* his brothers scoff, but even they cannot feel a little touched by the softness of their kisses, the gentleness with which he pulls her towards him. *Spoiling her,* and perhaps that is true, or almost so. Like all the rest, he buys her clothes, silk and damask and mountains of lace dating from the nineteenth century, but then he also buys her books: Brothers Grimm and Dostoyevsky, Anne Bronte and Hans Christian Anderson. Old, dark stories, fairytales and fae wrapped in innocuous silk and soft, worn leather.

And he buys her food: mountains of marzipan and halvah piled like colorful sacrifices before some ancient god, pomegranates bright as jewels and apples the color of sunset, roe red as blood served inside the bellies of the fish they were cut from. Ice wine in silver-ribboned bottles from Alsace; soft, snow-white sugar from the Saharas; the heart of a boar, served in a velvet casket; the tongue of a mammoth, cut by some lucky Mesolithic hunter and preserved through the centuries. Silver plates and ruby glasses full of wine: only the best for the best, the in-laws whisper, and lick their lips in anticipation.

Gracefully, graciously, Maria Petranov accepts it all, donning the plumed hats and velvet dresses in summer heat. They do not make her any prettier or wash away the age, but her husband looks at her as though she is made of diamonds and sapphires bathed in the sun.

In the visiting room, the women come, the women go. Jewel-bright eyes close on her, the new dresses and books on the shelves. Smiles and words always sweet but edged, as if disbelieving, as if waiting for something to happen.

Maria Petranov sits and smiles like someone with a secret, a banded bird perched amidst her captors, and she eats and eats and never grows less thin.

The sixth month, they begin to talk.

It starts in the bars, kitchens, alleyways—all the small places where the New People gather, with casseroles and giddy purple punch and cigarettes between their teeth. It starts with gossip, snatches of idle talk at art galleries, between mothers and grandmothers at libraries—*did you hear? Yes him, you were there, at the wedding—*

That boy? No, I haven't, but I thought—

Saw him just the other day—

What? All these months, and he still hasn't—

It is strange, yes, but then again, he was always a very strange boy. Some boys are, and that is to be expected—though, at any rate, glad that isn't *my* son there, stalling and mucking around. Too young, some of the older women cluck, and married off already; no wonder he was so sentimental about the whole thing, honestly, what were parents *thinking* these days. But there is no real fear. Nature is nature, and he would come around, in due time.

It is not until the tenth month that they begin to truly worry.

Three weeks and two days into the tenth month, they come to him.

It is a contingent of them—first sons and doctors fresh from residencies, tall, bronzed businessman and the wealthiest and most well-connected old women in the country. It is not necessary—he is young and by all accounts inclined to agreeableness—but there is a power in age and accomplishment, and it is rare that the rich and influential do not take an opportunity to display themselves.

It is early when they arrive. He welcomes them at the door, and takes them to the parlor. *Maria is out,* he says as he pulls out chairs, taking the porcelain teapot from the cabinet and the small crystal cups from their wrapping. It is a lie, but they let it pass.

He sits down. He pours them tea. He listens.

We have heard, an old woman begins, pearls around her neck and powder on crinoline-thin skin, *rumors, lately. And my dear, we are concerned.*

She pauses, watching him. When he says nothing, she continues.

I suppose you are fond of her, and that is a lovely thing as love always it, but there are rules, you know. You understand that, don't you? Even Isen and Eva had to part too, in the end. She was dying; he was not meant to be; there was no other way it could go, no way for them to both survive. It is sad, but that is the way it is.

A sympathetic smile. A hand reaching to pat his, brief touch of skin on skin.

And that, as you well know, is why we do this today, in their memory. This is our pact with the Old People: that we take their kind, one every year, and we join with them, for the renewal of both our peoples. Years before and us and years after, and this is what has carried us through. And so, my dear: this is your year. This is your pact to fulfill, your tradition to carry on. We have each our own place, each our own part to play in this scheme, and this is yours.

It is an honor, you know.

She sits back then, satisfied in what she has said.

They watch him, waiting.

Slowly, he picks up his teacup, gently swirls the contents between large hands. Slowly, brings it to his lips, sips; slowly, places it back down, last dregs of leaf slowly drifting together.

He says, very slowly and very calmly, *no.*

His guests glance at each other. It is not so much surprise as it is disbelief that passes between them, the clear sweep of incomprehension at the words just out from his mouth.

My dear, the woman who says after a moment, *I'm not quite certain—*

I am sorry, but I am certain. No. I won't do it.

In the silence, he reaches over and pours himself another cup of tea.

I'm sorry, another of the old women, gold rings and lace cuffs, says, *but I don't—*

No, one of the men says, shaking his head as he raises one hand, *No, let me.*

He stands up, patriarchal authority quivering in every inch of his frame, slate-grey mustachio quivering as he looks down at the figure before me.

Now. I know your parents, boy; they're good folk; respectable folk. They speak highly of you, tell me you're a good sort—smart, reliable. Type of kid who listens to sense. Now, I know that you younger lot have different ideas, new notions about equality and how these things should go. And that's all well and fine, I'm not saying there's anything wrong with that, but there's a way about these things, alright? They came first, all soft flesh from the mollusks and worms; we came after, from the volcanos and the crust beneath, and we were made of stronger stuff. Diamonds to dirt. Natural selection, that's what it is. Bird eats worm, cat chases mouse. The New People overtake the Old. It's biology, and you can't fight biology.

Arms crossed, face stern, he stares down at him, a king in a three-piece suit with every expectation of being obeyed.

No.

Still sitting down, still smiling that soft, bland smile. No inflection in his voice, no change of fear or worry in his eyes.

Excuse me?

I told you, he says, *No.*

Young man, another man says, standing then as well, *this is ludicrous—you cannot be possibly be serious—*

He stands up. They are large, barrel-chested men who tower over him, but he only stares calmly back, face as immovable as stone.

Wordlessly, he leads them out, closing the door behind them.

They do not come again.

Two weeks into the eleventh month, she comes to him.

He is sitting in the library, mouth a thin line as he stares at the book in front of him. He does not look up at her entrance, only continues turning the pages—slowly, carefully, each movement laborious, an effort of wading through suddenly viscous air. Hunched amidst the medieval furniture, fireplace light not enough to dissipate the shadows, he seem more like a statue than human, some stone thing carved into the shape of a man.

Love, she says, and her voice is a whisper, dry and charred and barely there.

He says nothing, does not move from in his seat. Flips another page.

Love.

No, he says. *No.*

Love, they're beginning to talk. We can't wait, not much longer.

I can't do it. I can't do it.

Hands on his shoulder. Soft, so small against wide brown shoulders. And her eyes on his: dark eyes, calm eyes, dark black on his reluctant green.

You must. Your people, darling—

They don't deserve you.

It isn't about what they deserve. It's about what happens and love, already, it's happening. An old couple, out walking in the park yesterday found themselves unable to move. Legs stiff, feet sticking to the concrete. They are talking about taking someone else, next of kin—not quite a replacement, but enough to hold on.

They can't do that. The ceremony is about choice, it has been since the first pact was first made, and if they do that—

Shh, she says, placing her hands over his. They tremble, slightly, and her fingers stroke his, soothing. I know, love. But they are worried, and fearful men will do strange things for a little safety.

You knew what you had to do, coming into this. You knew the rules. And it is almost a year now, love. Tick, tick. Time to do keep your promises.

In the hearth, the fire flickers once, twice. High above, something in the old house creaks, lost medieval ghost or rusted machinery in need of repair.

I knew, he says finally, softly. *I thought I did. I didn't want to, but I knew the stories and I thought that I would be ready, that I could do it. That, when the time came, it would even be an honor. But then you, you...* He shakes his head, staring resolutely at the ground. *I can't do it.*

My darling, she says as she leans towards him, straw brittle hair brushing his shoulders, lips hovering over his, I want you to.

He looks up. For the first time that night, he meets her eyes; and despite it all, the wide span of his arms and the hard diamond polish of his skin, he is just another boy, some frightened young lover impossibly smitten and willing to tear down worlds with it.

Please. I'll do—I'd do anything for you, give you anything, but this I just—I know what will happen if we don't and I don't care—anything but this. Please. I'll give you anything else you want, but I can't—I can't do this.

Oh darling, she says, smiling as she brushes hair from his face. I would never ask anything from you, when you have already given me everything I could have ever wanted. But you know what this is. You know it must be done. And, my darling, if you think it will make it easier, it is something I want, too. It was not all altruism that led Eva to offer her life to Isen; after all, she was dying too.

The fire crackles, between them.

Please, she says. For me.

He gazes at her, eyes dark and pleading. She gazes back.

And then his great granite shoulders heave, a soft slump of capitulation, and he looks up at her, still frowning but resigned. She smiles, encouraging.

That isn't fair, you know.

I know, love. Love and war, darling.

Slowly, he shifts his arms around her, and she settles against him, easing into the space he makes for her. Gently, she takes his hand, placing it against one thin, sallow cheek.

Maria—

Shh, she tells him. It's fine, you're fine, we've waited so long for this, darling. It's alright.

Tentatively, he begins stroking her hair. She leans into the touch, loose and languid, eyes slit like a cat in the sun.

My firebird, he whispers, petting her blood-and-ashes hair. *My soul, my sweet breath, my—oh, oh,* oh *my love—*

She leans down, face pressing towards his, and he kisses her.

He kisses her, and the kiss is fire and ice, it is the universe exploding into life and contracting on itself in the same breath. He kisses her, and her mouth meets his as well, and the touch is fundamental, atoms colliding in soundless space, the super-charged, elemental force of two bodies folding into one. One thin hand reaches down, tugging at his belt, and he can do nothing but obey.

Maria Petranov smiles, and something lights in her then as her mouth curves around his, sparks crackling across her body like struck kindling, and for a moment, she glows.

By the time he finishes, panting and sweat-slicked, hands pressing bruises into her hips, she is no longer breathing.

A week before the marriage, the darkest day of the year.

Two figures sitting on opposite sides of the same, small room. Between them, downstage center to their stage left and right, a collection of silhouettes: the proper representatives from each side and the appointed intermediaries who had seen this through many times before. From different families and peoples, strangers who would hardly acknowledge each other in the street, they have come here today to this place to witness this, make the ritual true.

They talk. It is a long ritual; it must be, centuries of tradition carefully lifted up and dusted to set the pact in place. A monotonous stream of words, setting out of official terms and agreements—words meant more to be said than to be heard.

At either side of the room, the seated figures say nothing, unmoving as they wait.

The legal officiant—middle-aged, balding, sharp-faced and dressed in his Sunday best—closes his book, nods at the gathered families. As Isen and Eva did meet, as blood and stone did intertwine, so we come here again, the end of another year and cycle of the sun, for the renewal of both our peoples. In accordance with our traditions and our histories, will you accept your part?

It would be an honor, Maria's father says.

Speaking for my family, his father says, we would be honored to accept.

The officiant nods, and then there is no more words to say, nothing left but silence and expectation.

She stands, then, walking towards him. A moment later, hesitantly, he does too. He is tall, a full foot taller than her, shoulders solid and wide as a wardrobe, but he is hunched now, suddenly young and unsure as he stands next to her, this fragile-boned woman with sharp dark eyes.

She smiles at him. She does not say anything—that is another thing that is tradition, contact both physical and verbal forbidden until the final rites joining their families together are completed—only looks at him, eyes steady and expectant.

He looks away first. Then, slowly, as if drawn by some inexorable magnetism, turns back to meet her gaze.

She is still smiling, and though her eyes are still sharp and dark, they are not unwelcoming. Slate but warming to the touch, metal malleable and choosing to bend.

And slowly, tentatively, he smiles back.

It is not much. A moment of kindness, reassurance given out of the natural instinct to comfort—but in time, it will grow, roots stretching and thickening to crack the foundations above.

They eat her on a Sunday, the day of rest.

Her family is there as well— grandmother and grandfather in wicker lawn chairs, mother and father at the table, the crop of younger children who screaming as they run through the grass. Three generations, brought together under one roof.

Her parents are at the table, tears quietly falling onto their plates as they reach across the table for more lemonade.

Such a good girl, her mother sighs. *Always so smart, even when she was little, you could tell—*

Her father pats her arm, face grim as he lifts another piece of veal onto his plate.

Across from them, the other family sits. New People adjacent but apart from Old: the way the seating has been has always been. Their pavilion is larger, bright-jeweled with clear wines dancing in crystal flasks: red and white and pink, blood and bone and bright flushed flesh. Dressed not in black but emerald greens and peacocked purples, rare birds come to some nineteenth-century ball. And, behind osprey-feathered fans and flutes of champagne, the whispers of a genteel aviary float—

(and such a scandal, such a good name and so many good sons before—)

(at least now people can stop writing about it thank God my daughter wouldn't stop talking about how romantic it was, can you imagine—)

(well you know what they say about youngest children—)

(and oh yes, how glad that isn't me, my son would never—)

And then there is him.

He sits at one end of the table, a lone figure in faded black wedding finery. His family sit by him there, brothers and sisters arrayed in gemstone colors. Parents on either side, several seats away—the distance careful, respectful. Traditional.

They do not talk to him. No one does, really. It is always a strange thing, the end of a marriage, and though this one has been stranger than most—they have all heard the stories after all, the rumors of the soft, quiet boy and the witch-woman who had wrapped lies around his heart—they leave him be. There is curiosity, but then there is still tradition.

They serve her heart on a bed of plums and winter blossoms, and if he feels any discomfort as he cuts into the red flesh, he does not show it.

It is a beautiful day. Under the blue sky, in the fresh sunlight, they eat and dance and talk, go all the business of living.

They eat Maria Petranov plate by plate—liver braised with sage and new potatoes, marrow spread over bread by tureens of pot-au-feu—and only then, when they are finished, bones dry and gnawed, do the guests begin to leave.

He stays. As the tables empty, the caterers come into pack up the pavilions and chairs, he stays, straight-backed and eyes fixed on the ground. The sun dips low and bloody, and still he stays, single black-draped figure simply sitting there, as the last of the day fades.

Only then, with the last of the light fading from the sky and the stars beginning to show, does he look up.

And on the other side of the table, dress the color of milk and new snow spilling over her knees, the girl sits and smiles.

For a moment—the blink of an instance, the space between exhalations—she is there, this fae creature in the shape of Maria Petranov, skin pale as cream and hair as red as sunset. Every part of her girlish again, young again, but for her eyes, dark and old and fond as she smiles at the man who had been her husband.

Hello, darling.

And then—like the flashing of a hummingbird's wing, the wind rustling through grass—she is gone, leaving nothing but a memory of fondness and the smell of spring.

 M.C. ASTER

THE MINOTAUR'S DILEMMA

From afar, the Minotaur may be taken for a bullock,
A gentle beast nibbling on petunias and daisies.
But with a tiger's teeth arrayed in his mouth
Any luckless vagrant straying into his
Cavernous maze—be it sheep or shepherd—
Learns the Minotaur doesn't like his meals
To chatter.

Like any Dark Lord, he likes a postprandial nap, but
He sleeps fitfully, and wakes too soon in his palatial
Stalls, to rage and to weep about mankind's abuse
Of his mythological status. His misery multiplies
When summer's crush of tripe arrives, scribbled by
Snotty—if eminently edible—brats, who mangle
His legend annually in their academically dubious
Book reports.

Alone in this bleak state of mind, this demigod
Suffers not only bouts of indigestion (he ate that
Whining whatnot just to shut him up), but must
Endure millennia of such indignities, never
Able to collect not a single drachma's worth
Of royalties.

Benjamin Niespodziany

HAT COLLECTION
for Zachary Schomburg

Look inside the lighthouse
for a man selling

hats. One hat like an anvil.
One hat like an attic. One hat

laughs whenever
anyone nearby cries

while another hovers
an inch above your head. The man

selling hats
inside the lighthouse

wears a lighthouse hat
that's not for sale.

Every day is a painless day
with a hat like that.

 GREGORY ARIAIL

HUNTING SEASON

If you enter the Smoky Mountains from a particular corner of North Carolina and pass beneath the right waterfall, you'll come to my territory, where a fragment of Alaska has fallen from the sky. The tundra laps up against my beloved crag, which I call Prospect Rock. Below me, the sliver of Alaska extends for a thousand square miles. From my overlook I can see, on the clearest days, the tundra's end and the twisted peaks of the Carolina mountains begin again.

I was a paleontology student in Asheville in my former life. The fossil record shows, quite indisputably, that this shard of Alaska fell from the sky: the petrified Sitka spruces, the salmon and muskoxen burnt yellow and black in the rocks. The clincher is the proliferation of tektites, tiny marbles of clay and glass, which show that this was an impact site and that a torrent of fire once overwhelmed this place. The fact that the land below my mountain is Alaska, rather than the remnants of a small, tundra-swathed planet, or a fragment of Siberia, is less provable, but can't be denied by those who have spent a summer or winter in Alaska and know its biome like a lover's home.

You must be very quiet in these parts, especially during hunting season—rainy, green, fragrant July up here on Prospect Rock and in the rest of Appalachia, but the rusty scarlet of October down there in the Alaskan tundra. During hunting season, the wandering mountain arrives like a migrating caribou. Minus ptarmigans, the arctic warbler, and a few bugs and grubs found in most regions of the planet, the wandering mountain is the last surviving creature in this liminal zone.

The wandering mountain is my predator, my prey, my enemy, my obsession. It embodies a state of being I can never accomplish—a perfect blend of human and mountain. Never, despite my great desire to fold into this beautiful landscape, can I achieve such a fusion, no matter how deep I bury myself in permafrost or how ardently I blaze a trail on the rocks with my glands. As I speak, the wandering mountain creeps into view from the east, a moon-tower with the topographic prominence of Denali. It's looking for a way out of this cage, seeking brother and sister mountains whose high, serrated, Arctic summits shred clouds and generate weather systems broad and powerful enough to swallow continents. How it came to be in this impossible place I don't know. All I know is that it's looking for a way to break through the encircling walls of Appalachia, whose peaks are much tinier than the wandering mountain, but which create a magical barrier it can't penetrate. What slaughter and geographic havoc would follow its escape?

My wooden foot and crushed, withered arm are the evidence of my only close encounter with the wandering mountain. Long ago it nearly detected the passageway to the outside world. I distracted it so that it did not discover and thrust itself into the opening, shattering the barrier's one weak spot and inevitably exposing this secret place, this Alaskan gem, to humanity's rapaciousness.

Nowadays when it crosses my valley it always moves slowly, listening for me. It disappears into the west, only to reemerge within a few days on its return journey. This happens once a year. Afterwards it migrates back east and I have to wait another year to end this game of hide-and-seek.

But hunting season has begun again and the wandering mountain is here. Will the stars finally align to give me the bait I require? Will I accomplish the goal of my life, to be alone and always alone, to think coldly and clearly as spring water without the ache of a competing consciousness?

Its flank brushes aside a cloud. It is listening. The wind swirls and the ground is nervous, trembling, hot.

*

I hear someone at last. My trap has sprung. The wandering mountain is on its way back east. It's perfect timing. A human being found the secret waterfall in North Carolina, entered the cave behind it, and is following the trail of emeralds, fossilized mushrooms, and arrowheads to the light at the tunnel's end.

I limp over to the cave's mouth, about a dozen yards from the hole in Prospect Rock that I call my home and hermitage. I stand in the light so as not to scare the person too badly when they exit the tunnel. I chew on my tongue to bring it back to life and run my fingers through my beard, combing out the leaves and shaking out the rock dust, untangling the intricate shafts and channels. It's important to be presentable and cause no undue wonderment.

I press a finger to my lips and hold it there dramatically with my withered arm flung outwards.

The figure that breaks through the cave's darkness is a man's. He stops dead in his tracks when he sees me. He is dark-haired, clean-shaven, and robust. He wears a red backpack and holds a mushroom fossil.

He watches me distrustfully, silently. Of their own accord, his eyes follow the direction of my arm and there, between the hallway of trees, alight upon the massive object slashing the sky in two.

"Not possible," he mutters. Curiosity draws him towards me.

"Come and see," I plead, dropping to my knees and continuing to gesture wildly at the mountain. "But please, whisper, whisper as softly as possible so you don't attract it. It's trying to get at me, to kill me." Tears run down my cheeks. "If it dies, I'll be free...and you'll be free, too."

Like a sleepwalker he moves towards the overlook, keeping his distance from me as if I were a beggar. At the cliff's edge he stops and studies the thing like a scientist. His breath quickens.

"It's just..." he whispers. He squints. "But it's moving."

I open my mouth to reply but he interjects: "Where is this? I'm lost, I was searching for Chicken of the Woods and Lion's Mane. This isn't Panthertown Valley." He fingers a red backpack strap.

I lick the mustache hairs hanging over my mouth and iron them out lengthwise with my fingers to speak better.

"Take my word for it, that mountain does move on its own—at a snail's pace, mostly, except when it's hunting. Then it goes real fast. Mind if I join you?"

He nods absently.

I come up beside him. I find myself mesmerized, too. The wandering mountain rises much higher than the encircling ridges, like a lighthouse amidst porcupines. It has a sharp, luminous, snow-capped peak. As it passes through the valley, probably at about five miles an hour, the dwarf shrubs and grasses warp and swell, moving out of its way yet making no sound. A faint smoke trails the mountain like heat waves on a summer day but it causes no damage to the landscape. It creeps across the setting sun. After a few seconds the world plummets into purple semi-darkness.

"There must be someone inside the mountain driving it," he says. "It must be a fake mountain."

'Oh it's the real thing. I haven't been around cities for a long spell, but I never saw a skyscraper of that size and girth. It's got trees on it and glaciers and those sedimentary stripes."

"And hunt?" he says a bit louder than he should. "Did you say the mountain hunts? What do you mean?"

"Here," I say, unlatching the blowing horn at my side. "I'll show you."

*

I scramble as swiftly as I can to my hole. I dive inside and close the lid of interwoven branches and crawl to my lookout spot, an irregular crack in the rock. The man stands frozen, glancing in my general direction but not seeing me, scared and mystified by what I've just done. My horn blast still echoes from cliff to cliff. The wandering mountain has stopped moving. It seems to listen. A slice of sunlight, like an orange peel, lies on its northernmost buttress.

Suddenly the mountain materializes right in front of us. Dusk washes over everything and wind blows the man over. He cowers, his arms wrapped around his head. It has taken no time for the mountain to cross the ten-odd miles between its position in the tundra and my hermitage.

Its ice-shagged cliffs tilt backwards until something, a little creature attached to the base of the mountain, appears, squirming up the naked rocks. It is no bigger than an infant. In fact, it is a kind of infant. A grey, bald infant with eyes of blood and the shadow of a prepubescent beard. Only its head, neck, and arms emerge from the mountain, like a snail emerging from a titanic shell. From afar, it would be as difficult to spot the infant as a grey candle flame at the base of a grey cliff. Up close, however, it magnetizes and hypnotizes the vision, so that the mountain erupting from its spine becomes a background as watery and vague as the landscapes of medieval portraiture.

"Are you the gatekeeper?" the infant asks in an gravelly, ailing voice.

I load my shotgun and aim.

The man says nothing. The infant shifts in and out of my sights. I angle myself differently, resting the barrel on a lip of rock and re-aiming. Stop trembling, I tell my hand, stop trembling.

"Are you the gatekeeper?" it asks again.

The man's black hair streams behind him. He is running. The mountain shakes a little. I hear a distant swoosh and before the man has gone ten feet he is buried in a pile of snow.

The infant crawls towards the pile, the mountain gliding behind it. It scrabbles into the snow like a fox. A curve of snow now blocks a clear shot. The twilight dimness makes visibility worse.

Slowly, the man's dark head emerges from the pile.

"There you are," the infant says.

"Please," I hear the man gasp. "I'm a father."

"But not the gatekeeper?"

"I'm a mycologist," he adds confusedly. "I'm Alex."

Then come the screams. A grey, webbed hand rises above the snow; a grey hook of backbone. The infant bobs up and down, chewing and slurping, only millimeters of its scalp visible.

Alex moans and whines and falls silent.

Finally the infant lifts its head into full view. Slabs of viscera dangle from its stone teeth.

I pull the trigger.

Its head explodes. The mountain leans backward. And farther back. It is falling. Falling over the autumn tundra. It happens in slow motion. I brace myself for an earthquake and an earthquake comes. Everything in my hole clatters and ricochets. The earth wobbles drunkenly.

Red sunlight fans out over the rocks.

I crawl out of my hole and find Alex wedged waist-deep in the snow. His clean-shaven chin and jawline have been eaten as well as his Adam's apple. His throat gapes wide open. Snow crystals and some kind of flaky mineral, perhaps mica, make his cheeks glitter in the dying light.

The great mountain lies across the valley, sinking its edge into the distant peaks like a sword.

*

Hunting season is finished. My enemy is defeated, made into God's tombstone. To honor Alex I eat his heart.

I rearrange my beard into its normal shape—the shape of a key with multiple channels, wards, and bits. I stiffen the hairs with saliva and rock dust. I limp over to the cave's mouth and with a heave shut the stone door. I get on my knees, crane my neck, and insert my beard into the serrated keyhole, turn it, hear the lock's tongue click, forever shutting the gateway between the Smoky Mountains and my own private Alaska. At last I am king of this land. The dream I stumbled upon in my youth I share with no other consciousness. The ptarmigans and blueberries are my treasures. The milky striations and brown eye-knots of the aspens beckon my tongue to them. Without a rival, there can be no anxiety, no perversion, no meanness, no bliss even—only this.

 Michael Stein

THE FLIGHT OF ICARUS

The myths handed down to us are filled with baseless assumptions. There is no other way they can be told. Without adding these in we would be left with names and ambiguous events, as if they were obscure modern poems rather than the very foundations of our culture. In lieu of this we add the embellishments to make the stories whole, to hold all the words together like the wax in Deadelus's invented wings.

So Deadelus is made to tell his son that the wax will melt at too great a height, an ordinary scientific observation which Icarus, in his boyish recklessness supposedly chooses to disregard. The moral of the story then is what? Listen to your elders because they know more than you? Or rather, temper your enthusiasms, for they might prove deadly? Or is the message narrower and more specific, that when you are in the process of escaping don't let your attention get diverted, not even by something as exhilarating as flight, or a closer proximity to the sun?

I don't believe for a second that any of these explanations arrive at the truth of that terrible fall. I can only imagine the words which passed between father and son as they ascended above Crete, though I think they must have had much more to do with the prison they were leaving behind and below them than with the physical properties of feathers and wax.

First, Deadelus gave a vague idea of how far they'd have to fly to reach safety. After all, it wasn't only a question of getting beyond the prison walls, but beyond the reach of Minos's' soldiers. And here is where the seed of tragedy is planted in the boy's head.

How far do you have to go to be free of the threat of imprisonment? Up in the air, the idea of confinement suddenly became nonsensical. There were no walls, nothing solid to keep you still. On the earth though, there were borders and barracks and armed guards. People were walled in cities, and those outside were walled out. Scanning the ground as far as the horizon, Icarus's eyes saw imprisonment everywhere. Even where there wasn't a fortress in sight he saw a clear potential for incarceration. At this point the mere idea of a room with a closed door made him shudder with fear.

So he flew upward, further up in the air, towards the clouds, towards the sun. Perhaps he knew his wings wouldn't hold, or already felt the air thinning as his lungs gasped for breath. The airy kingdom he imagined so vividly obviously doesn't exist, a place where prisons are an impossibility. But for those few moments of freedom, maybe the first such moments his life had ever known, Icarus was flying directly towards it, forging a path there, and no matter what you might say against it the truth is that he was never imprisoned again.

AARON ANSTETT

PLEA

Alexa, help me
decrease my surface area
then go live in sepia-tone cabin
on the label of bottle of Bourbon
in imagined, idealized Kentucky,
never a slave state nor home
to continued mountaintop removal
but birthplace still of Abraham Lincoln,
Loretta Lynn, Harry Dean Stanton, Muhammed Ali.

Alexa, from the cross-hatched chimney
trickles a scribble of wood smoke,
and through a window you see a thin and tiny me
reading in rocking chair, bottle on table,
image on label infinitely repeating.

Alexa, how many days left, not mine alone but everyone's?

Alexa, what shall we do or say to lessen suffering?

Alexa, when will we at last infiltrate the kingdom of heaven?

Alexa, how do we gain immunity from prosecution for our many crimes and sins?

Alexa, how can I and the entire extended human family
enter witness protection but instead of southwest desert
or Midwest suburb, different, better planet and/or dimension?

Alexa, a hummingbird in the orchard swoops from apples to peaches.

Alexa, please.

❖ ADAM PENNA

THE WIDOW AND THE COWBIRD

I

My real parents were brown-headed cowbirds, and cowbirds are parasitical. So one day my birth mother, seeing a stranger's bassinette unattended, laid me beside the sleeping baby she found inside. Then she flew away with my father to I don't know where. I never saw them again, but I couldn't have known that then, lying like a drowned spider beside the enormous human baby.

When the strangers who owned the bassinet returned, they found where once they had had one infant now they had two. Because they were responsible humans, they fed and clothed and cared for me and raised me as if I were their own though clearly I was not of the same species.

Against dishonesty in every way, my new parents never kept my origins a secret. Instead, they reminded me where I came from at every opportunity.

I suspected as soon as I could see that I wasn't like my brother. While he attempted unsuccessfully to crawl along the dingy linoleum of the kitchen in the small apartment we rented above a very nasty old woman, I flew from room to room with great ease. Though my new father would encourage flying, whisking me along with a broom, my mother's pleasure about such talents was more ambivalent. As I flapped and dipped and dived, she frowned and hissed at me and comforted my screaming brother against her breasts.

Other than this, I suppose we lived a normal life. Our family owned a dog and a cat (which threatened me day and night). We owned a television and a stereo, too. We owned a washer and a dryer, and a car and a mini-van, and we ate pizza on Fridays, tacos or Chinese on Saturdays, Spam for weekday lunches, cold cereal or runny eggs for breakfast, and, for dessert, my mother chewed up a mixture of grubs, earthworms and crickets into a gruel which, beak open, I'd gobble up directly from her mouth.

When I got to be school age, there were no more treats of this nature. I was a very poor student, so there were few occasions for reward. My brother on the other hand was bright as a star. He enjoyed ice cream and candy and cake for his academic victories. I tasted only defeat.

There were reasons for my inadequate academic performance. I was ill-suited for human education. For instance, when the teacher prattled on about geometry, I dreamed of perching on a sturdy bough to count the leaves. When she sang the alphabet to the other children, in that frighteningly nasal intonation, I imagined a stopped-up gutter I knew and in which I bathed from time to time. And when she counted from one to ten on her pink human fingers, I looked at my wingtips to contemplate infinity.

Physical education was another story. I was quicker, subtler and keener than any student in the school. I flitted from start to finish in the time that the starter pistol fired and the gun-smoke cleared. Yet my physical acumen proved to incite the gym teacher into profound rages. When he tooted his whistle at me, his face red as a poppy, I sang back without a bother. Sometimes he became so annoyed, I would flutter about his head with earnest apologies. Then he would become even angrier, until finally he would remove his sneaker and toss it at me. By the time the sneaker skipped across the pavement, I would be out of sight, hidden safely in the underbrush. It might take all afternoon to coax me out, and when I was finally convinced the earnest pleadings ceased and the disciplining began.

Because my cowbird parents had chosen to leave me in the care of a species I could not easily dominate, which is supposed to be the case, my brother eventually overcame me in every significant way. He graduated from school in a respectable rank and found a trade he enjoyed and plied it. After some success, he discovered a woman, for whom he felt affection, and he married her. They had two human babies of their own—named Skeeter and Crew—and lived in a house similar to the one we grew up in after we finally left the apartment above that nasty old woman. My brother and his family, I am told, have a happy little life. My little nephew writes me from time to time, and I am grateful for that.

II

My life didn't go as planned. I did not graduate. I did not find a pleasant career. Neither did I catch the eye of a mate, with whom I could couple. Instead, I fell into a wretched job at the mines, for which I was hired only after every canary in our county had died of asphyxiation.

On the job, I was a terrible success with my fellows. Often upon arriving, I heard my name echoing up from the bottom of the earth and throughout the caverns, and as I climbed the dank mineshaft in the evening back toward what seemed at times a silver moon in a pitch black night, I heard my name again thumping through that tight space like the whir of wings.

To the foreman, I was as useless as a paper pickaxe. For fun, he flicked me on the beak and cursed the day he hired me. I could only nod at his remonstrations.

During this time I hadn't a permanent home either—my adopted parents had long since slipped away south, like my biological parents, without promise of return—so I flew freely from tree to tree, perching on a single bough no longer than an evening. Inevitably the owner of that tree would come down in his robe and, with his paper rolled up like a pastry, shoo me away.

"Don't let me see you here again! You nasty little lay-about! You freeloader!" the owner would say, and the next morning, if he found me innocently perched in the same tree, though on a different bough, he would say, "I thought I told you to scat?"

"But sir," I'd say, "You said..."

Before I could defend myself, the slipper would be off and I would have to shoot up through the foliage like a bullet.

In winter, these instances were fewer. On occasion in the night, while I huddled against the dull heat of a branch, open to injury without the protective camouflage of the leaves, God released on the earth a dusting of snow that cloaked me well enough so I might sleep undisturbed until late morning, when the sun pulled back that insulating cover.

All of this I counted a mercy and a blessing and found to be quite pleasing. Even the soft tick-tick-tick of melting snow on the white mounds below the boughs seemed comforting like the precise, lulling of a metronome some mothers use to encourage infants to sleep, as my mother had done for my brother, and I on the bough warm with memory recounted in each drop how, on the sill in my brother's room, I had listened to the tick-tick-tick, felt the sun on my lids and waited for the first sounds of morning: a car coughing, a coffee machine sighing, a refrigerator door meeting with a kiss the warmer air of the kitchen.

Though food was often difficult to find, I never went hungry. In the neighborhoods, the lawns were pregnant most of the year with any variety of tasty insects, worms and seeds, though you risked your life to pinch a morsel there. Homeowners protect their lawns more fiercely than mockingbirds do their trees. In fact, eating from the lawns became so stressful my stomach upset me whenever and if ever I thought about feeding. I tended then to resign myself to the less satisfying meals of feeders displayed proudly in the yards of widows and fellow bachelors, especially when the dangers of the alternative felt too great or my stomach too tender.

One widow, whose feeder I frequented, also watched me bathe in her birdbath every evening when I returned from the mines. In the hour just before dusk, a golden web of light touches the treetops and I hopped up her driveway onto the lawn to eat from her feeder. From the lip, I spied her at the window, humped in a robe of terrycloth and topped with a red bandana. Just come from the mines, I was all black and sooty, coated with an oily sheen of earthy stuff, which seemed phosphorescent in that dimming light. To the widow I must have appeared, at first, like a grackle minus the piercing yellow eye, but stepping out of her bath, the day melted away and my tough brown head revealed, she saw the species I am. I suppose it was the transformation she enjoyed and which led her to invite me to tea.

III

We sat in a Florida room, which jutted off the kitchen like the peninsula after which such a room is christened and in which I had often seen the widow silently watching me eat or bathe outside on her lawn. She poured me a large cup of tea filled with sugar and lemon and served me, too, a plate of biscuits topped with jelly.

Sitting in the plush lap of her enormous indoor/outdoor furniture, I felt vulnerable. I thought that I could be crushed, but when she sat across from me, I noticed, as she sunk into the chair, that despite her large robe, she was frail and small and could not without considerable effort rise to harm me. So I gobbled up the food and gulped down the tea, which soothed my stomach so completely I felt almost instantly repaired.

"You are a strange bird," the widow said. Her papery hands struggled with the teacup. "I've watched you in my birdbath now for some months, and I have never noticed you acting like the other birds. You come alone. You eat alone. You bathe alone. And should the other birds taunt or torment you, you seem not to take offence, but simply flit to some high bough to wait for those small bird consciousnesses to lose interest, so that you may return to your ritual. Strange, indeed. At first I felt shock at your behavior and wanted to shoo you away. Now I feel otherwise. I think we're much the same, bird."

A great friendship grew between the widow and me. Every evening when I finished with my bath, she invited me in for sweet tea and jelly biscuits, which I devoured as she spoke of things she had done, wished she had done, hoped yet to do though knew now that she was so close to the end she would probably never do.

She hadn't any family left. Her husband, whom she supposed she had loved, was dead eight years this winter, and her children, a daughter and a son, had moved out to the West Coast and visited very infrequently. For my part, I would listen quietly to her stories and musings, and if her focus waned or if her story trailed off into regret, I drew her attention to the plaintive whines of the catbirds or the mournful songs of the crickets.

It wasn't long before the widow offered that I should live with her, which seemed to make great good sense because neither of us had anyone (I had told her my story piecemeal over time), and cohabitation in her experience relieved the tedium of loneliness. I said it hadn't in mine, but I was willing to try. So we searched in her attic for a cage, which had once belonged to her pet canary before it was conscripted to the mines and subsequently perished. Then we set the cage, airy and roomy and clean, on the dresser in her bedroom. She lined the floor of the cage with newspaper and hung a perch for me to swing on and a mirror for me to gaze into and a dish for sugar-water and a dish for seed, and every evening before sleep, she read to me the books her husband had once read to her to help her fall asleep, and when the light went out, it was my pleasure to conjure up the moon in the window with the sweet birdsong I had heard from the beginning and all my life in privileged bird dreams.

IV

Because of the small regular pension the widow received—thanks to her late husband—I was able to quit my job in the mines. We had money enough, she said, and it pained her to think that I, too, might die of asphyxiation. She had suffered the deaths of her husband and her canary. She would not suffer mine.

The way she presented the case, you might think my leaving the mines was a favor I should perform for her. But this offer was unsatisfactory to me. There had to be some recompense for all that she'd given me. Otherwise, I would come to feel like a freeloader and she to resent my presence. I could not abide that. So, in exchange for room and board, she agreed to let me sing sweet high-pitched tunes while she gardened in the beds around the Florida room or while she washed the dishes each evening in the tremendous sink. Further, she promised to wash me once a week in that same sink, and when she scrubbed me under my beak, I cooed and kicked until the suds nearly filled the kitchen.

One day I said to my widow, "Widow, are you happy?"

She was planting nasturtiums in a window box. Her hands were sooty with the rich potting soil.

"I am, bird," she said.

"Do you know how I know I am happy?" I said.

She paused from her work and turned to me. The sun shone on her face and, when she visored her brow, a long shadow veiled her eyes.

"I find myself singing sometimes when I'm alone."

"You are a strange bird," the widow said, "but then I guess I'm a strange bird, too."

"Then we make a pair of strange birds," I said.

"Indeed, we do," she said.

She returned to the nasturtiums, and I to song.

That evening, after my bath and hers, she kissed me lightly on the forehead. Later, while dreaming, I felt the place where her lips touched me burn.

V

Summer ended. Autumn arrived. The days grew shorter and shorter. Then nights longer and longer, until it seemed we lived most of our lives in darkness. The trees dropped their leaves, and the sky exchanged that golden web of light for soft pinks and violets. But still my widow and I were happy, and though we spent most of our days that winter indoors, rather than out in the garden digging through the beds, still she bathed me and, after I was dry, kissed me on the forehead, where all night that kiss burned.

It was the most pleasant burning, and, as I slept, I dreamt of faraway places, exotic places, like Morocco or Fiji, where the boys and girls ran naked in the streets, up winding alleys or along the beaches, whose sand was soft and warm, and the birds there reflected all the colors of the prism and bore strange names, which resembled incantations in the mouths of the people. But even then there must have been that restless spark, buried deep in the belly of the cottage, threatening to escape, perhaps from the furnace cage or from under the hot water heater, where the pilot light coiled like a snake.

Late one night, I woke to find the bedroom engulfed in flames.

The door to my caged was locked, and my widow sat at the foot of the bed. She stared into her lap, her hands folded there like two fish in a pan. I began to call an alarm. Could she be asleep? Could she be in a trance? Could this be my dream?

"Widow! Widow!" I said. "Is this what comes of happiness? Is this our reward? The winter was almost ended. The trees are bare, yes, but look even now the snow shrinks from the cottage... Don't despair, please."

She looked up at me, my poor widow. She had been weeping, I could tell, or else this was a dream and she was melting.

"These were the happiest days of my life, bird. But now it's dark, too dark, and though the snow steps away from the cottage, I look at the empty trees and know... What will we do, bird? If I could I would return to when my children were little. I bathed my son once as I now bathe you. And my husband... He would kiss my cheek while my hands were submerged in the suds—vanished!—and my baby boy cooed like a dove. But they are all gone now, and though you no longer work in the mines, someday you will go, too. I don't know how. I suspect I'll find you at the bottom of that cage some morning, your feet sticking straight into the air as if bracing yourself against something terrifically heavy. Then what will I do? The life of a bird is short compared to the life of a widow, whose years are measured long and long, like afternoons in the rain. She watches trees uproot in great storms! Would that our lives should burn up, and you and I with it, than wait to discover what grief the future holds for me..."

"Please, widow," I said. But then I stopped and began to sing a quiet, mournful song. I'd forgotten myself capable of such sadness, but there it was, rising to the surface again, like a she-whale and, beneath those tones, those sorrowful notes, something else accompanied, a calf perhaps, following his mother over the horizon.

My widow looked at me. Flames flickered all around her and swallowed up the curtains and the furniture. Small figurines slumped over on the dresser top. The bars of my cage grew so hot they glowed red then white then...

I ended my song.

"Widow," I said. I felt no urgency. The song had cured me of whatever fear I had been feeling. "Widow, I've known sadness before and, like you, I'd rather not return to it. But before we burn up here, and my wings become flames and I shed these black feathers to put on ones of brighter color, as if this blackness were fuel, I want you to know that this place, this oasis, has been the only goodness I have ever known. And being that, I think, I couldn't have found a better life. I mean, I don't know that I would have recognized it after the glory of this summer. All else would seem dull by comparison, less brilliant, and I guess the danger would be that I wouldn't know I was happy at all, and that is no less than never having been. So. Let me out of my cage. I won't attempt escape, but rather I want only to perch on your shoulder there and sing into your ear, until I can't sing anymore, the flames die down and all that's left are embers and ash."

My widow rose from the foot of the bed. Her satiny nightgown billowed and reflected the fire in the room. Though the bars were white hot, my widow lifted the latch, and I was free. She didn't flinch touching the hot bars. Rather, she lifted her two fingers to her lips and rubbed them together.

'Come," I said. "Let's wait. It won't be long..."

She resumed sitting, and I perched on her shoulder. Closing my eyes, I began to sing. This wasn't the same song as before. It was different. I had never heard it, and I suspect now that it was the song of the oldest birds, the ones who gave up the sea for the air to become symbols, like sacrifice, for something higher and greater and lighter than that which swam below the surface or walked through the undergrowth.

As I sang, I felt the heat of the flames on my eyelids. If I hadn't known better, I might have thought I was looking straight at the sun. If it had ended there—my love affair with the widow and this world—I think I would've been satisfied. But then something I did not expect happened.

The sun went out, doused it seemed by a wave, and I thought that I had died and continued to think so because what burned incredibly hot a moment ago seemed to me now cool and wonderful. It was as if we had stepped together through a door or had dove into a pool and, all at once, what was a sensation growing more and more fierce and terrible, like a hungry prowling cat, consumed itself in its fury and was devoured.

I opened my eyes.

"What happened?" I asked.

My widow laid me down it the wet, brown leaves. Flames engulfed the cottage, the roof caved in, but we had escaped and lay hidden safely in the woods behind the house.

"I couldn't do it," my widow said. "But don't think it was your song either, silly bird. I found the strength to rise only after resisting that song, though—because I don't want you to think your role was insignificant—I didn't set out to rise, but as if in a dream, the more I tried to close my eyes the more I found that I could see, and so the more I resisted your song, the deeper and deeper it settled in me, and then I rose and now we're safe."

She lifted me up between her palms and brought me close. She kissed me on the forehead. Her lips were cold, her face streaked with soot and tears. I was no longer burning.

"I've gotten us this far," she said. "Now what will we do?"

I couldn't answer. The moon shone big and bright through the bare trees. The boughs glistened. We fell asleep there on the ground, huddled against one another, shivering like animals.

VI

The next morning, I woke before the widow, very early. The sun glowed low behind the black trees and glistened there. I had heard that night, while dreaming of ice skating with my widow, the sound of hooves moving softly through the dry leaves. It seemed so faint and small and far away that I might have mistaken and dismissed the sound for insects gnawing on the core of a fallen limb. But when I opened my eyes, I found a doe and two fawns nosing through the browse a few feet from where we lay.

The mother lifted her head, assessed me and, deciding I was no threat, returned to browsing. Then I fell back to sleep—it could not have been more than a few minutes, really—with that image burned in my vision. I continued to dream about skating on ice, but this time, at the edge of the pond, there stood the doe and her two awkward fawns, whose legs seemed as if they were uneasy on ice, though their hooves were buried in powdery snow.

The fire had consumed most of the house. What remained smoldered in a heap of ash and soot. A wispy tail of black smoke spiraled up into the wide blue sky.

"Widow," I said. "Wake up!"

She began to stir. Her limbs were obviously stiff. The flimsy nightgown, which the flames had licked and singed, provided little cover. Still, she smiled enthusiastically when she saw me and stretched and yawned.

"I'm awake. I'm awake, silly bird," she said. "What is it with you? Why are you so excited?"

She was correct. I was excited. The house we had been living in no longer stood completely, and where it did, it did skeletally and starkly. I could make out the charred remains of our old life: the kitchen utensils and appliances, our headboard, a buckled mirror. The once white refrigerator was black now, and the door swung on a busted hinge.

There was more, too. My cage hung on its hook in such an attitude that it seemed as if it were a torso been struck by an arrow someplace delicate and painful. To look at it made me shiver.

The widow surveyed the site.

"Oh dear," she said.

I snapped to. Could she have seen what I had seen?

"What?" I said.

"Pardon?" the widow said.

"Nothing," I said.

"What now?" she said.

I decided not to tell her about the deer and her offspring. I think in general, even between the most intimate mates, it's best to keep some secrets close. Besides, if it were a dream within a dream and I told her, she might panic or, taking the vision as a good omen, feel unreasonably assured. At this point, we couldn't afford excessive delight or despair.

The next day—we didn't waste time—we traveled to a distant preserve located on the island. There, we had heard, visitors came only infrequently during the summer months to walk the trails. There was the threat of hunters, whose guns shook snow from the trees, but the danger seemed minimal, if we kept our distance. No foolish hunter would risk hunting a widow, and I was much too stringy and small to make a meal or a trophy.

We set up house, a primitive looking bower, beside a salt marsh, which had frozen over. Beyond the limits of the marsh, we could make out the slow ferries gliding across to the mainland, shouldering aside bright floes in the blue water.

My widow had never suffered the elements like this, not as I had before she had taken me in, so this arrangement, however temporary, was toughest on her. She bore it relatively well, though. She kept a small fire burning always, but far from the dry bower. During the night we'd huddle together and listen to the cold wind whistle soft, strange music through our makeshift shelter.

It was quite beautiful and haunting, the melody we heard, and it influenced the strangest dreams in me, dreams of places whose names I couldn't pronounce, where women dressed as brightly as birds with big sharp talons and moved in ritualized dance, slowly, deliberately. I assumed, even there in the middle of the dream, that these movements were too particular and too precise to have been learned. They must have been instinctual, part of the muscle's memory, the communication of sinew and ligament and bone made visible to some peculiar end, of which the mover was completely or, at least, partially unaware.

VII

Our good luck didn't last long. Soon my widow caught a fever. I covered her with grasses and reeds, the little scraps of this or that I could find and what feathers, now that I was molting, fell from me or I could pluck, until I seemed more naked mole than bird. Yet no matter the measure I took, my widow became sicker. She coughed and shivered through the night and swooned during the day. She couldn't rise to feed herself, so I was forced to feed her mouth to mouth as mother birds do for chicks. This helped some. I don't know whether the benefit belonged to some character particular to the insects I chewed or to some element contained in my saliva, but she seemed as if she might begin to recover, for a time.

The effects of the concoction were short-lived. Soon my widow was suffering more terrible deliriums and hallucinations than ever. She cried over and over again that the hunters were coming for her. That the guns echoed through the naked woods only added to her agitation.

"I was afraid, bird," my widow said to me rising from a fitful sleep. "I thought I would outlast you, but now it seems you will outlast me. And our marriage, certainly sanctified somewhere holy, perhaps holier for being so far from what the common call sacred, makes you a widower. I know what you'll be facing, then. It is beautiful. You will doubt it, but resist, because it is. And now I know how worthwhile my time alone, a thing of winter, was because this last late summer bore the best fruit. I lied to you, bird. It was your song that made me rise. I always found myself born again in your throat. When you called my name, it was magic. If I didn't know better, I might believe (am I so very old?) that after, when I'm buried or eaten by animals, your song might stir me from sleep again, and I'll leap like a cricket from the cover of grass into your beak like food. Do you think we're always so wrong, bird? Do you think we always, while alive, fear the wrong things? I do. Then (and I've just come to this), if this is true, let it be that death, if nothing else, is a coming to fear the right things and regret only what we failed to do in this life meeting us in the next like an old friend. What a chance that would be. I'm tired now, bird. But I'm not so very cold anymore. The fire feels good on my face and the bower you made keeps out the cold well enough."

There was no fire burning.

The bower whistled sadly where the wind entered. There was nothing left to do now but wait. The widow coughed and turned to sleep. We were deep in the night. I didn't have the throat to answer or sing or weep.

I cursed myself for ever having come indoors. What had been wild about me, what fluttered off into the woods when cars passed or children came too close, my instinct, my ability to survive cold and wind and rain amounted now to nothing because it couldn't spare the one thing I had loved in the world. I couldn't suffer this for her, and I hadn't the wit or talent to guide her through. If I'd ever known, that knowledge was lost to me now.

Happiness had taken it from me, and if asked then, when I was happiest, would I trade this for that, I would've said no, but I wouldn't be so hasty now. I knew what it meant to be tame. It meant to be mortal and know it. There was nothing I could do. I'd been her pet. The life of a pet is a good one, until it isn't. Then there is the regret and knowing that that regret is not only part of being alive like this but an integral part, too.

I wondered suddenly if my parents, my real parents, ever regretted leaving me in the care of another couple. They couldn't. It was their nature to leave me, and they followed it. No regret can come from that. Neither could they regret leaving the numberless brood of brothers and sisters, those other orphans, with whom they littered the world. I hoped none of them were ever captured and given as pets to some loving family. The grief would be too much. It would overcome them utterly. Some grief would be better left undiscovered. But perhaps this is true only of other people's grief. Our own we cling to as if it were itself life or the last root before a terrific drop.

VIII

The answer came to me in a dream. Before I could fully understand what I was being asked to do, I was on my way. When I returned, my widow was still sleeping.

"Wake up, my love," I said to her. "I have something for you."

"What is it, bird? I'm tired. I was just dreaming of the most fantastic place. You were not there, but I felt your absence like a terrific pang."

"Listen. I had a dream last night, too. But you were there. You met me on the banks of this marsh here, but the place was not frozen. Everything was alive and well. You pointed out, as we moved through the sedge, various roots and leaves and stems, which have healing properties. Then there was this one dead place. You warned me not to go there. You said that it was a place from which I would never return. Some risks, you said, and sadly, too, as if your whole being would crack, are not worth taking. But I've returned from that place just now to tell you that you were wrong. It is worth the risk. I found there, in that place, a cure for your sickness. I can't take the credit for it myself because I believe that you weren't as sincere with me, in my dream, as you might have been had we been awake. I know enough to know that this is the case with dreams. They say many things at once, while we can only say one thing at a time. Or perhaps it is the other way around. I don't know, and it doesn't matter. Here drink this."

I had made her a tea from the roots I had found. She sipped the tea.

"It's very hot," she said. "It's nice."

The next morning, I woke before my widow and loosened myself from her embrace. (We slept very close to keep warm during the long, cold night.) I crept out. It was late winter. The trees were bare and black. A fine, powdery snow lay atop everything. The sun hadn't risen yet, but neither was it completely dark. It seemed as if a net had been cast over the preserve at once blue and some color far from the palette of creatures. It was warmer than it had been in months. The air was pregnant with an earthy scent, not quite fecund but promising fecundity.

I hopped down to the edge of the salt marsh, as was my ritual, and alit upon a reed, which nearly buckled under my weight, though I'm certain now that I couldn't have weighed very much after so hard and cold and scarce a time.

It was a spectacular view. A flock of migrating Canada geese flew overhead startling the silence of morning. My heart leapt from my chest. We had made it through the winter. Our suffering had not been without reward.

The sounds of the geese must have awoken my widow, who crawled out of the bower to join me.

"What is it? What is it?" she said.

Now the sun shone over the long black line of the distant shore. The sky brightened only there. The first ferry lurched from the slip and began to cross, and my widow reached up to where I perched on the reed, seized me as gentle as one might an egg, and cupped me between her palms. I knew, however healed she was, it was still too early for her to be walking about. But I could say nothing. Something caught in my throat. I was singing. I was singing again.

"Shh!" my widow said, "the world isn't yet awake," but I couldn't stop for happiness.

 KAILEY TEDESCO

AT THE BOTTOM OF THE LAKE, A FAIRY TALE

with the handbell swallowed, my evil wilts like a grandmother visit.
    baby's breath dries above the dark water in our memorial —

you may drink of myself, from myself, blood spillage
    breadcrumbing the cups of my hands.

on this tour of my double-jointedness, my past thumbs
    plum-thrust in pie. all of my past cavities

loiter in cupboards, well-rotted from their own lack
    of having eaten. i'm birthmarked

in green eggs — their mold coronates my head, snipped clean
    with its tiara of flies. everything, yes everything,

will absolutely green in its sick. i carry wine baskets
    through the forest & still grandmother rough brushes

the sins from my hair. in the lake, there is a future-corpse
    & evidence knows this. grandmother keeps

severed fingers in her good hand for luck, leeches feeding
    their bleed. i scry the blood-let, a spill

on the surface, my breath kept safe under a rock
    at the edge of the beach.

SARAH KAIN GUTOWSKI

A PENDULUM'S SWING

So she swings from the rafters—recycles the rope
from the boats and ties a noose around her neck,
finds a bar stool to stand on and then kick away,
laces the other end around a beam and its brace,
pulls to check resiliency, whether the wood will hold
her weight. Everything appears as it should.

My ordinary self remains removed, apart,
sequestered inside the house, attending to chores.
She feigned a kind of nonchalance when saying
her final goodbye, a second time, the gesture
absurd as snow in June. It's November now,
and the season's creep has hastened to a crawl,

frost eating at the window panes, the creak
and pop of glass and wood expanding every time
she raises the heat. She turns up the radio, too,
tries to drown out her imagination, the sonic ghost
between her ears: a different kind of creaking,
a pendulum's swing, our extraordinary self dangling

above the garage floor concrete, her shadow
an impermanent stain no one will have to clean.
My ordinary self tries to stop her mind, but
it keeps arcing toward the garage. *We're better
this way*, she says to no one, or perhaps
to Savior Cat, who figure-eights around her feet.

 LILY HOANG

FILLED-WITH-GRIEF

There once was a boy who would one day become a king. The royalty in his blood was not pure, and, as such, it could only fail in its perpetual battles against despair. It might be said that the boy's blood was as regal as it was dolor—a heavy blue, cerulean pitch—but that was not his problem. If anything, the boy did not have problems that might cause sadness: he had a mother who adored him and an old spinster to dress him. Once, the boy had a father, and it's true that his father was the king, but the boy hadn't been told the rest of the story, and either he was too much of a coward to ask or he didn't care. Regardless of reason, no one had promised him any lengths of happiness in the first place. The only part of the story the boy knows was that when he and his mother arrived at the old spinster's wooden home nearly seven years ago, he was only a baby, and it was the old spinster who named him. She named him Filled-With-Grief.

*

Here is what happened before: The king was at war when his wife, the queen, was pregnant, and although of course the king wanted to be present for the birth of his first child—whom he very, very secretly had hoped would be a girl, and he wanted to name her Pyrus because had his mother not been stealing pears from the king's garden late at night, they might never have met—war is war, and a good king becomes a bad king if he never leaves his throne. Shortly after his departure, the queen birthed a perfect boy, crying and red and full of farts and burps and all the things that might to anyone else seem disgusting but to a new mother could only be interpreted as wonder and grace. Letters of congratulations and news were sent to the king, but war is war and always submissive to the devil's whims. And so it was that the queen and her new-born son had to flee. Her son was tied to her back and a cloak was tied to her neck by the finest silk ribbon, and they ran.

They ran, knowing neither direction nor hope, and an old spinster found them tangled in brambles and thorns, too frightened to cry out for help.

"Let me help you," the old spinster said. "Give me your hand. I will pull you free."

At this the queen, whom the old spinster did not know was the queen, much less her very own queen—imagine, if you will, a day before Google, before information and identification could be verified, before fingerprint scans and databases: our story occurs many ages before even the first electricity had been made—said, "I would, believe me, but I haven't any hands."

Although this was hardly a time for semantics, questions were answered and a plan was executed, and the queen and her son went to live with the old spinster for seven years, and for seven years, Filled-With-Grief was not so much sad himself but the grief that filled him belonged to his mother, it fell loose from her skin, in the particles of each sneeze and each sigh, out of her body and into his, and although it's true that royal blood is strong, Filled-With-Grief was only a half-breed after all, his mother being of common stock. Still—she was beautiful enough to woo a king, despite her lack of hands.

*

Too many things happened before. Let's just say before she was queen, she was a common girl, a beautiful but common girl, and although her father loved her very much, he took an ax and chopped off her hands.

Something about the devil, if you believe in such fairy tales.

*

Not all wars are Trojan Wars or World Wars or even Wars on Terror. Some wars end. Some people survive it, and the return home is long and delayed and full of treacheries—but one must always acknowledge the good fortune of survival, rather than focus on the pettiness of travails. Our good king, victorious but haggard, returns from war—slaying challenge after challenge, thinking only of his baby who by now must be a child. The king tries to count the years of absence, but alas, time was only standardized during the Great War of the twentieth century, which is many centuries after the war our good king has just won. Indeed, back then, there were not even grandfather clocks ticking along, only grandfathers with their elastic memories and grumpy snores, both of which are inadequate measurements of time.

The king returns to his castle and what does he find?

His most trusted servant brings him a box. It's a gray box, metallic. The servant bows and thrusts the box out towards the king. "As you had demanded, your highness."

There's the smell to the box, and it's a smell the king knows immediately: the rot of human, the deterioration of human flesh: it's different than other dead things, and within a war, it is the only smell that exists, its pungency can overpower orchards of blooming cherry blossoms. It's a smell that lodges itself, both within the moment and for every moment that will follow until it is your own body that has become rotten, at which point it is no longer a problem because its familiarity has neutralized itself beyond recognition and you're dead or so near to death that recognition no longer exists. The king will not touch the box. "Take it away," he says, and he allows gravity to take his body down.

"Your highness!" the servant screams. "Help! Help! The king has fallen!" And in his fervor, he drops the damn box and its contents roll out: two hearts, one the size of a small woman's fist, one the size of a large walnut still inside its shell; and four eyes.

And suddenly, the king lifts himself, not quite to his feet—the king is only a man, after all, and he has just fought a war and trudged his way all the way back to the palace—and drags himself closer to the box and its scattered contents, these shriveled marbles of organs. He breathes in hard and relief glides through his blood.

Soon thereafter, the king learns that the servant received several letters detailing how the queen and her changeling child must be murdered, by decree of the king, for the crime of birthing a changeling. The king's letters, worded with fury, demanded his trusted servant perform the task himself and keep the queen and her changeling demon baby's hearts and eyes as proof. But the servant couldn't do it. Instead, he sent the queen and her non-changeling baby away, strapping the baby to her back because she had no hands of her own, and fastened a cloak around her neck, and put the hearts and eyes of some simpler animals inside the box. The servant had assumed that by the time of the king's return—if the king was victorious, not that the servant lacked faith in his king, save for his cruel and unorthodox command to kill the queen and newborn child and save their hearts and eyes as keepsake, which were orders that the servant knew were divergent from anything the king would actually want—the organs would have shriveled to stinky, indistinguishable balls.

But, of course, the king could smell the difference, and bothering only to change his clothes and trim his beard, the king departed immediately in search of his wife and child, his queen and his prince.

*

It doesn't matter how he found them.

It doesn't.

For seven long years, the boy was filled with grief—but now, he feels something, something not desperation, nor despondency, nor woe, nor depression, nor sorrow, nor misery—the list could continue, but let us suppose you get the point. The boy feels a whole new emotion, and he doesn't know what to call it. And, of course, he needs a new name.

Everyone is happy. But a name is a curse like any other, and one day, the boy once known as Filled-With-Grief looks out the gilded window in his glorious castle. Now he is king and has a wife of his own and a son and two daughters, one of whom he has named Pyrus, having heard the story so many times before. Everyone is happy. Everything is beautiful. He lifts one leg over the window's ledge and pushes off, as if to fly.

 STEPHEN DELANEY

OUR PLACE IS IN BETWEEN

Our bodies fold in, making our outer hides stronger. Folded once and we're fist-tight, firm; eight and we're arrow-proof and solid. But your efforts don't end—cigarette ends, mad dogs, Lysol—and so we fold up tighter...

Eventually common sense whispers we're safe. Yet no, we're not safe. Your methods, though crude, are compulsive. A rock pounded long enough will weaken the toughest layers. And though we call you slow, because of us you grow inventive, sharpening your wits on our fears. Rocks give way to thick sprays, misting machines, green fumes that reach out long tendrils to choke the tight nooks where we hide.

You'd think we'd be glum, yet our lives don't lack for joy. Like you we've been shaped by the struggle. We've found that folding, properly done, can give us great pleasure, hours unburdened by your world. And enough folds and our inner eye opens, can see every angle, every unflattering view.

Yet a life spent recoiling has a cost. Sunlight seems harsh to us, the ground too coarse for us, and these days it doesn't take much to make us fold. You in a dimming house—a cigarette's orange glow. A dog-child's silhouette at night. Pine-scented Lysol wafted by a fan in the den. And your thoughts invade our dreamlife: Weapons inside us jabbing out. Dog-boy whispering we're kin. Being set aflame, our ghosted selves—the selves we could have been once—silent as they whisk up and fade.

It's our dreams that cause us grief now, for sometimes they make us unfold. Whether from confusion or some latent need, we put ourselves in danger, unfold in a street where we've been tossed, or a crude pen where we've been piled with those we once loved.

If one of the dog-children—*your* children, though you disowned them—is nearby, it might approach us, then, with its teeth, gently lift us and carry us to the caves where we're safe.

But sometimes you're waiting and we unfold right in front of you. Our skin loosening, expanding with sighs, cracks that grow louder, until what's left is this naked warm belly— rising and falling, creased but soft as yours. Manna from the god in your sky.

 Dan Raphael

HUNTER'S MOON

Too much wind for a week, now stagnation alerts, the plants—
withered, discolored & abandoned—have declared it winter
a few still bright, some won't shrivel til snow or freezing rain
maybe next weekend some showers, later a second sun
or the old one with new quantum innards

Full moon in a week, the trickster moon, which may not show up
or could keep getting bigger when it's supposed to peel away—
a game of outer space chicken with the earth too distracted
by internal crises to get out of the way or scream

What's the calendar underground, in the root network
are there alarm clocks or sensors, we've spun so long
stopping would be disastrous, disorienting, not falling
but walking with different muscles, talents the feet and knees
never expected, the hips dominance unwillingly revealed

Skin holding its breath, a hood that zips over my face
must trust my guide dog app, windshields as tinted as the rest,
if it can't be delivered i don't need it, easier to insulate
myself than the house—if i could get my van into the living room
i wouldn't need to go upstairs, sealing it off with submarine doors

Slowly the roof retracts. walls aching for their original colors
seeds & crumbs long encarpeted so impatient for the first rain,
threadlets of micro-lightning fogging into channels commercial free
and not from anywhere we can get to or map, as if the world stopped

and i kept going, molecular momentum, shedding skin and structure
not sure how much ground i can cover and still get back
a brief organic prism, bait for i'm not sure what

 Matt Schumacher

THREE REVIEWS: A TRIPTYCH OF FANTASTICAL FICTION IN TRANSLATION

Paul Willems. *The Cathedral of Mist.* Cambridge, MA: Wakefield Press, 2016.

A playwright "whose refuge plays evoked mysterious places, junctures of the known and unknown,"[1] Paul Willems, the countryman of Henri Michaux and praised as "the last of the great Francophone Belgian fantasists," also composed fictional prose obsessed with the ineffable. Willems frames these eight tales with an imagination and elegance that recalls the style of Italo Calvino. Plans for a palace of emptiness, or narratives born from spontaneous invitations from a Count to a chateau in a Finnish forest seem most at home here, as this writer is comfortable amidst terra incognita. Steeped in what Lorca designated the *duende*—authenticity, irrationality, earthiness, and a wisdom emanating as if from a goblin familiar sitting on the artist's shoulder, persistently reminding the artist that he will die—these dreamlike stories tantalize with their archetypal eye for the beyond, combined with an earthbound, undeniable melancholia. In "Cherepish," after a character named Hector asserts, "Dreams, too, are dress rehearsals, whose only purpose is to prepare us," he proceeds to share his dream of a huge ship which signifies his death. Later, a monk shows Hector a secret ossuary for martyrs in the mountains, as if it is given to him to visit "the gates of oblivion." This collection truly pursues epiphany, and the church in the forest conjured in the breathtaking title story, built by the architect V. who, "after years of meditation, renounced the use of stone" to instead build an edifice of fog, finds just that—the cathedral of mist manages to be many architectures, many surfaces at once: with vaporous naves and apses spun from the dusk, it is its own stunning creation, both a potent metaphor for the artistic process and for the ephemeral fabric of ecstatic spiritual encounter, as well as a symbol for the unknowable.

---

1   Donald Friedman. "Spaces of Dream, Imprisonment, and in the Theater of Paul Willems." World Literature Today. Winter 91, Vol. 65, Issue 1.

Amparo Davila. *The Houseguest.* **New York: New Directions, 2018.**

A literary figure of such magnitude Kirkus Reviews deemed her a "Poe for the new millennium," the late Mexican writer Amparo Davila wrote entrancing short stories of the uncanny and fantastic. Finally available in lucid, sparing English, these fictions ensnare readers from the first page, establishing deep atmospheric moods and psychological tensions. Plot twists first slightly unsettle, then expand the dimensions of fear, the author's most consistent theme, alongside insanity, menace, and death. Though her stories resist simple interpretations and mastery, her female protagonists face distorted, extreme versions of everyday problems readers will identify with. Davila's characters in these twelve stories include a wife tormented by her husband's mistress transformed into a giant toad, a female narrator whose diary records her attempts to master suffering as an art, the houseguest(a "grim, sinister" figure "with yellowish eyes...that seemed to pierce through things and people"), and two demoniac undefined figures, Moses and Gaspar, who the protagonist inherits from a deceased brother, and who poison a benign apartment until it's a claustrophobic, sleepless nightmare laced with unease. Serious readers of the fantastic should find these stories better than the rarest night terrors, nearly impossible to resist. Carmen Maria Machado has called Davila's tales "equal parts Hitchcock film and razor blade."

Marcel Schwob. *The King in the Yellow Mask*. Cambridge, MA: Wakefield Press, 2017.

Marcel Schwob, to whom Jarry dedicated Ubu Roi, influenced Ernst and Borges, proofread Wilde's plays, and wrote academic essays which recognized that fifteenth-century vagabond jargon had been appropriated by the poet Francois Villon.[2] What comes across clearly in translation after over a hundred years is that this erudite French Symbolist writer whose fantastic tales were written in the vein of Gautier and the French Fantastique is a writer of innumerable and dangerous talents. Schwob's gift for historical setting and detail is a marvel. His gift for effortlessly evoking mysterious lost places we wish we could visit is everpresent, as in this first sentence of "The Blue Country:" "In a country town I wouldn't be able to find anymore..." Readers may find themselves suddenly moved by the despair and plight of silent salt smugglers and maritime crooks from the 17th century. Such potent historical detail grounds these fictions that readers will be caught unprepared for the unexpected eruptions of the fantastic. Unpredictability is one source of Schwob's powers. In a sudden flash, his characters may meet cruel fates; consider "The Milesian Virgins'" first sentence: "Suddenly, without a soul knowing why, the virgins of Miletus began to hang themselves." The title story, with impeccably realistic detail, depicts a masked king afflicted with leprosy who is the first in his line to face his family's legacy. As translator Kit Schluter posits in the afterword, despite its encyclopedic nature, Schwob's fiction "expresses a sense of genuine longing" and "explores a vast spectrum of emotions...he wrote without judgment of his characters, and perhaps it is exactly that which allowed him to achieve such unseen heights of terror and pity in their expositions."

---

2   Daniel Heller-Roazen. "Appropriation: Back Then, Inbetween, and Today." Art Bulletin. Jun2012, Vol. 94 Issue 2, 178-179.

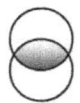 # SIMON ANTON NINO DIEGO BAENA

FEAR

I keep an eye
on the window

hearing
the creaks

grow louder
waiting

for the moon
to arrive

with urn
like silence

the portrait of the virgin
and child

that I never prayed to
stare at me

as sand drips
inside the waist

of an hourglass
it was my sister's

gift to herself
reading Lorca

in isolation
for one whole year

my face avoids
this antique mirror

when it rains

 ELIZABETH HOWARD

MOON BABY

Stepping down from the windowsill like liquid light,
swollen, staggering, hands twisted up like vines,
you tumble into my heart, teeth white and misty.
O slippery one, I have watched you softly descending,
the embers of fire in your eyes, too soon
the night is calling you back to its side,
messenger of stars, treacherous, ethereal,
your body like a snake uncoiling.

You unwind spools of stars, tell me
it's tedious, the skin on your hands cracks
and blisters. What sort of ointment
do they have up there for bleeding fingers?

Don't be fooled, you say, it's cold
and hard. The world is all edges
and vast plains of glacial white,
so cold it burns.

My teeth break the skin—
it's tough and sour. My eyes
water from the bitterness.
Kiss me! Kiss the tartness
from my lips, moon-baby,
swallower of seas.

I have seen you at night, lips pale,
hair unwinding—all moon.

ABYS

Abys had a look that was uniquely hers, my mother said. Then she contradicted herself and said, "She had a unique look for each person." On our living room floor, I rolled onto my back, trying to understand which was true, red shag carpet threads towering over me like ancient trees.

Listening to stories about Abys hurt. Like swallowing a handful of the unsmoked cigarettes my mother'd abandoned to her ashtray, which I'd tried more than once to capture her attention. I'd stay home from school when she seemed to wake from a long trance, in one of the rare moments I could look into her eyes, to study the colors, when they were brown or green, to discover something new, undefined. Usually, cast from the TV set, a legion of soap opera characters occupied them, marched back and forth on the pupils' black screen, guarding my mother, like I always wanted to.

She claimed to have never met Abys, but the precise details in her stories made her so vivid that many women choked our living room. Many different versions stood around, cigarettes and pipes and hookahs clouding the air with smoke, all eyebrows arched in disapproval at my mother. When I attempted to put them together, to form a single person in my mind, the effort felt like an army of untrained boys trying to conquer a mountain fortress, one defended by starving mercenaries. Still, I'd inch closer and closer to her, trying to catch air from smoke.

When I was 12, in the middle of another quiet summer, I decided to search for Abys at the Zoo. My mother told me she had grown up in a small town, not unlike our small town, I'd assumed they were the same (one summer, after years of dedicated silence, I received her call and returned home to help my incapacitated father. My mother had grown eager to talk, to offer me small, literal details, as if she hoped to add tiny weights to crush down the many versions into one coherent story. Ventura beach, she said, during the Depression, near the railroad, Abys. As if the problem wasn't that I'd always believed them all and would like to forget each, however different). My matchstick legs carried me from our faux middle-class farmhouse, my shoes sparking flints against the sun-sucked black top. Our dogs and cats—we had two labs, one white, one chocolate, and two calico cats—followed me until they lost themselves in a frenzy of barking and stalking the smells of lilac and urine from boys who pissed in our town creek.

When I reached the Zoo, a seedy apartment complex known for drugs and prostitution (which I associated with the loss of family since I had spent time here with each of my brothers before they escaped home when it had been a smooth field of red dirt and perfumy, numbing manzanita) each of its windows burned with a different sun. Heat. Something had reached up and slicked my fingers, my palm. I pulled away. A sidewalk vent from the complex spat up steam. A sharp sting bit my bladder, an ambiguous, incessant throbbing, like a hand inside me stirring. I looked around for someone who might let me use their bathroom, but the buildings seemed abandoned. As I stood there feeling alone, I imagined each small apartment stuffed with boys, dozens of us herded to a kitchen to be packed in boxes, columns of boys stacked beside themselves, stored for deployment. I peeked through one of the windows to see if my intuition was right (this will sound improbable, but as a child, my mind caught glimpses of things, of undisclosed, shy places; I wished this capacity away until it atrophied and withdrew somewhere else). In the living room, five boys were doing pushups in front of a sun-glassed man who sat in a laz-e-boy chair, a man whom I intuitively thought of as the General. He wore an eclectic uniform that mixed fashion sense from different military branches. I began to sweat, or notice the sweat, on my forehead, my eyes burning, or beginning to burn, the space between my lips, a leak.

I banged on the door of the closest apartment. A woman with calico hair and a yellow crayon robe leaped out, her face blurry, like its features had been smeared with Vaseline, or clouded by a puff of smoke. Her chewing lips grew distinct first, the lipstick an unnatural color that I liked, a lilac that over the summer sometimes seemed light blue or darkish purple or white. For a moment, there was a sincere look in her eyes—the irises neon jellyfish outsmarting a murky ocean—that made me feel safe.

Abys gulped something down, grabbed my belt, and yanked me. The door's latch clicked behind us and she sat me in front of a mirror-top coffee table. Paintings of fish on the wall surrounded us—goldfish, piranha, squid—a hutch of kitschy ocean figurines—whales, penguins, sharks, waves, palm trees, lobsters and crabs and an abundance of wax parrots, parrot bookends on top of the bookshelf, parrot lovers on the fireplace mantle, a fireplace full of glittering sand. A needle gunned through my bladder, sewing together unfamiliar parts. My hands covered my barking, stalking lap. Abys ignored my discomfort, and asked if I would like some lemonade or tea or Coke or juice or water or beer. My eyelids grew sweaty at her suggestion, and I closed them, hoping to wish the images away. When I opened my eyes, she inserted a cold glass in my hand. Murky chocolate milk. It was seeping in my hand, or leaking, like there was no difference between glass and milk. A tiny puddle slicked my palm, a growing froth. I didn't want to drink anything but Abys gave me her death stare, and I noticed a new color, a hazel brown, take her eyes, and I felt sad for her, for a reason I didn't understand. The image of a porcelain toilet full of splashing milk and chocolate syrup swirls filled my mind. Feeling a little weird and a little scared, I took a drink. My throat tightened, and as I choked on it, Abys nodded, praising me and urging me to down the rest. The full feeling inside my body, not pain or pleasure, confused me, and grew. I had to let go.

The empty glass smacked the table and left a crack in the mirror. Abys ignored this, and the broken shards the accident produced. Although this didn't seem to bother her, I worried that she would freak out when she smelled the growing puddle at my feet. The double release had made me shudder, and in the mirror-top, my sweaty face—eyebrows knotted, lips sucked inside my mouth—struggled to identify itself in the ambivalent aches and spasms. I looked up to see if I'd been caught, and watched as Abys's eyes shifted color again, from hazel brown to hazel green. Her face had slicked too, and she seemed deeply pleased, I thought, perceiving my lack of control as the purest compliment.

She picked me up from the couch, slung me over her shoulder, and as my urine dribbled down her arm, she began telling me an obscene story. As we left the living room, I caught sight of the whale figurine in her hutch, which seemed to move, its lips shifting from a grin into something wider, or something smaller.

In the bathroom, Abys lowered my pants and aimed me at the toilet. Her hands seized me, squeezed like a trigger. More and more urine shot out, and she praised the size of my pistol. Feeling a surge of pride for a moment, then a stinging awkwardness that restored my earlier discomfort, I sought to escape the divergent feelings by shifting my sight to the bathroom window, where I found that nearby apartment again: through its window, five new boys stood in a lineup against the wall. The General, now sporting thick-lensed spectacles that reminded me of a magnifying glass, ordered them to underdress. He calculated, with a shimmering device, the length and width of each boy bicep, wrist, finger, leg, calf, thigh, etceteraetcetera. As the General announced official measurements to the group, each face suffered to remain quiet, straining to conceal its tears or triumph.

Afterward, Abys carried me to the kitchen, sat me on the counter and gazed into my eyes. I read in hers, which had gone completely green now (I asked myself repeatedly if they had ever really been any other color), total adoration. A response like this from an adult was a revelation to me, and despite my previous confusion, I was willing to do anything, no matter how pathetic, to sustain the attention. Abys fetched two bowls: one full of peanut butter, the other chocolate chips. She handed me a spoon and explained her technique:

Abys's Mixing Rules:

1) Dip spoon into peanut butter until fully slathered, a peanut butter spoon;
2) Remove spoon and dip into chocolate chips until fully slathered chocolate chip spoon (the peanut butter should be completely hidden now!);
3) Alternate between bites of chocolate-peanut butter and drags of cigarette.

Abys demonstrated the procedure for me. It seemed simple enough. I was excited to smoke my first cigarette. When I reached out for the spoon though, she slapped my hand and picked me up again; cradling me, she carried me back to the couch. She returned to the kitchen for the bowls and placed them on the mirror crack I'd made.

Abys sat down next to me and nodded once, indicating I should dip the spoon into the peanut butter and chocolate. I did. Abys lit her cigarette, and I waited to see if she would hand it over so I could take a puff. Instead her eyes lingered on the expanding smoke trails in the air. With the heavy spoon in my hand, I inferred those chips might fall off, so I reached out for the cigarette. Abys slapped my hand, took a long drag and then shoved her lips into mine. Smoke filled my mouth, and I started coughing.

Abys brought more dishes, placing them all around us, on the couch, the table, the floor. Chocolate milk, a meatloaf slice, orange juice, a bowl of scrambled eggs, two slices of pumpkin pie, a carne asada burrito, a vanilla shake. I didn't want anymore, but I wanted to please Abys, who left again and returned with a bowl of chili and a five-foot cheese board and arranged them in front of me like a tableau. I stared at it; Abys stared back. She gave me a thumbs up. The Merlot cheese looked good, and I thought I might get drunk if I had some, so I cut slices from the wheel, including the purple rind, and mixed them into the chili until they melted. Then Abys shredded cheddar cheese and we mixed that in and then we mashed crackers in.

Days of Our Lives was on Abys's TV. The camera shifted to do an extreme close up on the face of Dr. Marlena Evans Brady, psychiatrist heroine, a character my mother and I had spent many summer afternoons watching quietly together. Her contacts had a cheap green demonic tint. She was talking to herself for the audience, monologically extolling the merits of her grand plot to topple her once-beloved family, which she would accomplish by seducing and marrying her former archenemy, the notorious Stephano Dimera, a crime boss who controlled a vast network of mercenaries, who had recently kidnapped and brainwashed her with mind-control drugs and subliminal videos until, in this weakened state, Satan possessed her.

During the commercial break, Abys marched into the kitchen to make popcorn. I heard a can of kernels rattle into an oiled pan. They ratatatated as she shook it back and forth, then cracked open like shots from a firing squad. Before *Days* came back on, she dropped a huge drippy bowl of corn into my lap, and my overwhelmed fingers swam in butter and salt, gathering up oily handfuls. After I finished, a few hard kernels lurked below a buttery pond, and I put one into my mouth to suck the flavor. When I took the clean kernel out of my mouth, Abys told me to put it back in, at once. Hey, stupid, I made that, you're supposed to enjoy it, she said. I bit down but it was too hard and wouldn't break; instead, it ground against my teeth, rattled and dented until my jaw ached. Abys gave me her death stare, so I bit down harder until I heard it crack.

As my tooth and jaw throbbed, the room seemed to flood with smoke, and then the only thing I could hear *and* see—I know that doesn't make sense, but you can't blame me, I was in some pain—was Abys's voice. The imagery, the setting around me shifted one more time, like a camera cutting to a black movie screen, which then lit up to display an ocean and sandy shore, a beautiful scene from a beach. The camera, I guess, then panned down, mimicking the movement of someone's head plunging, and brought into focus an image of my socked feet running down a paved boardwalk. My head, or the camera, rose, and I smelled salt air and then passed a sign that said Marina Park, Ventura. The grass seemed jaggedly cut from the hot sun and the palm trees' big fronds made them feel like giant lurking flowers. My body ached, and I wanted to stop running but my legs sliced through a trail of alleys until I came out on a city street, then to Raymond Theater. My hand removed a nickel from my sock and set it on the booth's counter. I could finally breathe in the big dark room and pretended not to exist and had forgotten again to see which movie was playing. On the screen, King Kong reached out for Ann and my body felt sort of jumpy, so I wiped my hands on my dress. After the movie, I hid under my seat waiting for the next one to begin. This was the safest way to spend the night when the mercenaries came. An usher's flashlight woke me and I returned to Surfer's Knoll where I planned to sleep out on the sand, which is a good warm place to sleep even with the Santa Ana wind and I imagined walking out on the water with Ann and running really far out so that we could try scratching a hole in the moon, to see if movie things felt real, to see if touching them could save us, but then Kong's black and white hand emerged from below to take us.

I was a lucky because we lived at the beach. But we lived near the railway too, so the mercenaries could find me when they stopped for rest. They travelled across the country, traveling in loud, glimmering cars for weeks and were exhausted when they stopped and my parents asked five cents for a night's rest, and before they came to my room, I escaped through a hole I'd made in the wall. Kong's hand crushed us, Ann and I, placed us in his mouth and inside the train car, the mercenaries oiled objects like guns and drank and smoked and ate food from dented cans.

Abys held the popcorn bowl out to me, urging me on. A handful of kernels floated in the butter. My jaw and stomach ached from the first kernel, and I couldn't eat anything else. Abys stared at the TV, with the bowl in her lap, silent, for the next half hour, watching the end of the show (Marlena had begun floating into the air above her bed), and I felt guilty, like I had severed our connection. I tried to think of something to do, like an idiot, and asked Abys about the plot. She gave me a brief death stare, and then I sat quietly and watched Marlena who, by the way, had stopped levitating when her husband John Black, a priest, entered. But she did it just to fool him.

The rest of the summer, Abys made all kinds of things—shrimp cocktails, spinach dip, chocolate chip cookies (these were made of chips where the dough functioned as spackling), nachos, hot dogs, lasagna, stir fry, sushi, charburgers (hamburgers with melted cheese hidden at their center), and hot fudge sundaes. It was delicious, but when I finished my sundae, my stomach began to ache, like someone had gut punched me. I ignored it and we continued on—Marlena seduced Tony Dimera, Stephano's good-hearted nephew, urged her traumatized patients on to acts of vengeance, transformed into a black panther to stalk her victims, and finally, morphed into the form of her rival, Kristen Dimera, in order to take control of John Black and Stephano's empire—with cheesecake, vegetable soup, enchiladas, turkey with dressing and giblets, and fudge peanut butter pie.

One afternoon, after a mouthful of peanut butter fudge, I bit down on something hard, something that cracked in my mouth. I spit the thing into my hand and saw a popcorn kernel. Over the previous few weeks, my stomach had an ache after meals, and then it began to ache before meals. Bloated from constipation, a distended spot had purpled my belly, had grown like an angry seed, a seed shaped like a fist. Feeling paranoid, I rubbed the spot below my shirt so that Abys couldn't see. It was an unprecedented event and I couldn't predict what she would do. As I secretly rubbed the ugly thing, Abys prompted me to finish my pie. I said no, then waited to see what she would do. Abys turned towards the TV and started woofing her pie down. She grabbed my unfinished slice without making eye contact and stuffed it down, chugged her coffee and then mine. Then she turned the TV's sound way up so that I knew she was angry.

Now when Abys brought food in—cream corn, mashed potatoes and gravy, fish sticks, rice, tartar sauce, broccoli and mayonnaise, balut—I inspected it for kernels. When I discovered not one kernel, but a bundle in each serving, I suspected that my constipation was caused by a bezoar. I stopped eating, left unfinished platefuls. Abys ignored them, the plates piling up everywhere, the stinking smells, and when plates fell and broke on the ground, she'd quietly clean it up, then bring another serving. Whenever Abys went in the kitchen, I would pull my shirt up to inspect my bezoar, to see if my fast was helping to clear it, to cleanse. No, never, the ugly purple spot remained; in fact, it grew, despite the measures I'd taken, to the size of a real fist. Of course, I was hungry, too. I would stare at those heaping plates and come close to scarfing it all down, but then the fist's ugliness, the pain it caused, reminded me to control myself, to focus. I'd have to come up with a plan soon, I knew, or I'd need to eat something and grow sick, or I'd need to starve myself and die. Eventually, Abys caught me with my finger pressing down on the fist, trying to squish it. The spatula dropped from her hand and she pulled my shirt down, then untied her apron. She tied it around my belly, explained that her "natural" treatment would make it go away.

She continued to bring food to me, too, although each time I refused. Omelets, roast beef, fried chicken, prime rib with au jus and horse radish, donuts, waffles, collared greens, kale, string beans, salads of baby lettuce, Thai eggplant with purple basil and ghost peppers, arugula, Kouign-amann, carnitas, pickled walnuts, barbacoa de cabeza. Abys's dedication to her natural treatment grew more intense. She tied a homemade quilt around me, a black tie from a tuxedo, seashells, coffee filters, a Western-style denim vest. During all of this, I began to feel dizzy and fatigued and to sleep during the day. While I dozed on and off, I could hear Abys setting plates beside me, and the smell of heavy meat, desserts, and columns of rotten food.

Sometimes I found myself sitting up on the couch awake, not knowing the time, not remembering when I shifted into that position, with my fingers unconsciously rubbing the fist. I would feel completely disgusted, rubbing the ugly thing until it felt sore. One time, as I sat there staring at myself, I noticed Abys had left one of her lighters between a couple of old plates of food, now plates of playful grubs. I grabbed the lighter and flicked it to see if it still worked. It did. I stuck my finger in the flame and liked it, this burning. I began to imagine how good it would feel to light myself up, to stay awake in this feeding. I wanted to remain conscious so I could feel myself changed by something living, a spark. In a different form, smoke or ash, I could escape what happened, escape this ugly thing. I untied the natural remedies. I intended to undress and set fire to every inch of skin, to warm up, to change each part. Seeing my reflection in the mirror though, seeing the fist reach out, as if it were in search of a target, I looked different than I imagined. I piled the remedies on the mirror and lit them up.

Running away from the Zoo, the sound of cracking glass made me fear an arrest warrant. Our dogs and cats rubbed my legs when I reached our property. A light, excited feeling came over me as I opened the door. Although everything looked the same outside, I expected something new in there.

A cigarette smoldered in my mother's ashtray. Her eyes held the TV. I sat down next to her on the red carpet and looked up, eager for a talk.

"You fat little killer," she said.

DAVID SURFACE

THE SKIN YOU WERE BORN IN

A father's job is to teach his son how to be a man. That was a task I felt unqualified for. I know what a man is supposed to be. But what a man *is* is still a mystery to me.

When Daniel was two days old, right before they released us from the hospital, the doctor told us it was time to give him the ring. I suppose I'd known this was coming, but I hadn't thought about it very much. Like everyone else, I thought it was the right thing to do. Monica, however, did not feel the same way.

"It's barbaric!" she said.

"Oh, I don't think it's that bad," I said. "Everyone does it."

"I don't care what everyone does. He's our son. We can do whatever we want. Why do you want to subject him to something like that?"

I don't know how I talked her into it, what combination of words and reasons I strung together. I remember saying something about how I didn't want him to feel strange when he was around other boys, that I didn't want him to feel like a freak. And I believe I really meant it. But when they came to take him away and asked if I wanted to go with them, I said no. No matter what I'd said, I didn't want to watch them do it. But I heard it. From all the way down the hall, through closed doors, I heard Daniel scream, a terrible, long scream of pain and outrage that went right through my chest like a spear.

When the nurse brought him back to the room and handed him to me, she pulled back the blanket and showed me the brand new, bright silver ring that passed through the skin of his chest, right over his breastbone. She gave me a little vial of antibiotic ointment and told me to dab the place on his chest five times a day until it healed.

Monica wouldn't do it. She'd stopped talking to me. So I dabbed the wound on Daniel's chest five times a day like the nurse had told me to do. I couldn't get over how bright and shiny Daniel's ring was, compared to my own dull and tarnished one. I couldn't remember the day when I got my own ring, so I hoped and prayed that Daniel wouldn't remember this day either, that he'd forget all about the pain and how I'd failed to protect him. Like I told you, it was a job I wasn't prepared for.

They say no mother can sleep when her child is crying. It isn't true. I've seen Monica lie in bed like a dead woman while Daniel shrieked and cried in the dead of night. It wasn't always this way. For the first four weeks, she'd wake and nurse him, and when that didn't work, she'd walk the floor until he fell asleep in her arms. It was a beautiful thing to see, and I'll admit that I was jealous. Not of Daniel taking Monica away from me, but of the beautiful bond that the two of them seemed to have.

One night, Monica told me she was done.

"What do you mean, *done*?" I asked her. "Done with what?"

"With this," she said, handing Daniel over to me.

At first I thought she meant that we'd trade-off these nightly sessions, the way we'd always done with other tasks. But after a few nights, it became apparent that she had no intention of ever taking over this particular task again. It was mine now.

I suppose I should have been angry, or at least objected. But I didn't. I loved it. I loved every moment of it, walking with Daniel's little head pressed close to mine until it felt like our thoughts were passing back and forth between us. It was the most beautiful and perfect thing I'd ever felt.

As Daniel grew older, every night before bedtime, I'd read to him. It was, without doubt, the best part of my day, diving deeply into the stack of favorite books that I kept nearby on the bureau. I loved reading aloud. I used to read to Monica as we lay side by side in bed, before she became tired and wanted nothing more than to go to sleep right away. So this nighttime reading with Daniel felt like a gift, a return to the way things should be. Daniel would sit on my lap and help turn the pages, the top of his head just under my chin, until he grew too big to fit there, and his head rested against my right cheek.

Our favorite book was an old copy of *Fairy Tales of the World*. I loved it's heavy thickness, its musty-leaf smell. The illustrations were wonderful; watercolors, woodcuts, and pen-and-ink drawings by different artists, all dead now, their peculiar visions preserved in the yellowing pages. One of them, Daniel's favorite, was a Japanese demon or ghost in a long, traditional kimono, its face an elaborately grimacing snow-white mask framed by a wild mane of serpentine black hair. The demon, fierce and proud, wielded a long samurai sword over its head. I think it was the sword, more than anything else, that attracted Daniel. When he was eight years old and Halloween was a week away, he brought the book to me, pointed to the picture of the Japanese demon, and said, "That's what I want to be."

We worked all week on that costume. I knew Monica had a Japanese kimono-style robe covered with red and gold flowers—not the writhing dragons worn by the demon in the book, but close enough. I went to the costume store and bought white and black makeup for Daniel's face, and a black fright-wig that I teased-out with a comb until it flared-out like a lion's mane. A gold-painted plastic samurai sword completed the effect. When we'd finished putting on the costume, it was amazing. Daniel looked proud, fierce, and beautiful. It felt like this was the way he was always meant to look. He stood in front of the mirror, stunned at first, then energized by his own transformation, roaring and slashing that plastic sword through the air so fast and hard, I could hear it hum.

When I dropped Daniel off at school, I saw gangs of other boys dressed in khaki, camouflage, and military green, their faces hidden by knotted kerchiefs or black ski-masks, plastic machine guns and machetes clutched in their small hands. Daniel stood out among them like a phoenix among crows. I saw him hesitate for a moment, and I wondered if he felt the same misgivings that I did. Then he ran and joined the crowd, and the big school door closed behind him.

When I returned at three o'clock to pick him up, the big doors blew open and out ran all the other boys in their green, brown, and gray uniforms, roaring and barking like wild dogs.

When Daniel finally appeared, walking out of the school by himself, his wig was gone, the kimono torn open and hanging from one shoulder. His make up was half rubbed-away, the skin beneath it red and raw-looking. I got out of the car fast and ran to him.

"What's wrong, buddy?" I asked, going down on one knee and putting my hands on his shoulders.

"They...they laughed at me..." he gasped between wrenching sobs. "They said...I looked like a girl..."

I wanted to say *you looked beautiful*, but I couldn't because of the raw pain clutching my throat. It was the hurt of seeing my son wounded inside, pure rage at the ones who'd hurt him. And the knowledge that I was responsible; I was the one who had put the flowered robe on him and tied it around his small waist. I was the one who'd put the wig on his head and painted his face and sent him into that den of little killers. For the second time in his life, I had failed to protect him. And unlike the first time, this was one he would remember.

I think this was when Daniel began to change. It started with his voice. I could hear him trying to make it sound more grown up—not so much deeper, but harder, forcing the gentleness out of it.

One morning I found Daniel standing naked in front of the bathroom mirror, looking at himself. His small body had already started that almost imperceptible process of lengthening, of stretching out toward the future. I saw him glance downward, and I knew he was looking at his ring. It gleamed silver-bright in the bathroom light. As I watched, he reached up and touched it with the fingers of his right hand. Then he looped one finger through the ring and slowly pulled on it, stretching the skin over his breastbone outward. A pang of alarm shot through my guts, and I almost called out for him to stop—then he let go of the ring, and the skin at the center of his chest slowly relaxed back to its original shape. As I'd stood there watching, it felt like I was about to see something terrible and miraculous, something beyond my powers to describe.

I suppose I could have taken Daniel away from here a long time ago, before he turned thirteen. But thirteen always felt like such a long time away.

My neighbor Carl says that what kids need is a stronger sense of direction. In our town, that direction is very clear, but it's not for everyone. Every year, we lose another family, the ones whose boys are about to turn thirteen. My neighbor Carl says those families are the ones with *the wrong mindset,* and he's always glad to see them leave. *Good riddance. Keeps the gene pool pure.*

Carl spent some time out East, but came back here because he didn't like the *mindset,* as he called it. "They tell their kids, *you can be anything you want.* That's where the trouble starts."

One day when he was eleven, Daniel came home from school with his lip bloodied. He didn't cry when he told me about the boys who'd beat him up, but he wouldn't look me in the eye. I told him he didn't do anything wrong, and he glared at the ground like he didn't believe me, like there was something down there that he wanted to hurt and kill.

"Everything okay over here?" I looked up and saw Carl standing at the edge of our front yard. I explained what had happened. Carl looked at Daniel who had gone over to a nearby tree and was beating it with a stick. "How old is he?" Carl asked.

"Eleven."

Carl watched Daniel who had dropped the stick and was wandering away, kicking at clumps of grass on the ground. Then he looked at me. "You've talked with him, right?" Carl said. "You've told him all about it?"

"Yeah," I said. The truth was, I had not told Daniel anything about what was coming. Of all the serious talks that a father is supposed to have with his son, this was one I never wanted to have. I told myself that he probably knew anyway, that he must have heard stories from his friends at school. Like Santa Claus, or like sex, it seemed impossible that he didn't already know.

Carl glanced back toward Daniel who was still lashing at the tree with his stick. "You think he's ready?"

"He will be," I said. I spoke with that same voice I'd started to hear coming from Daniel, the voice of a man trying to sound stronger and more confident than he really is. *He will be.* What the hell did I mean by that? How was he ever supposed to be ready?

I wasn't ready when my time came. My father had tried. He'd made me join the football team at school when I turned eleven. We ran every day in the hot sun until we fainted, then the bigger boys held me down and beat me in the locker room. *That's nothing.* Those were my dad's words when I told him about it. So I never told him again. When I turned twelve, he started tying me to a tree in our back yard with thick ropes, saying that if I didn't want to starve, I'd find a way to get out. The first time, it took me a whole day and night, and I'd rubbed half the skin off my wrists and arms before I finally sat down and ate my cold supper. The next time, he tied me tighter.

I never did those things to Daniel. That was one thing that Monica and I agreed on. It wasn't because I thought that measures like these were cruel, although they were. It's just that I never believed they would help when the time came.

On my thirteenth birthday, they'd come for me at midnight, appearing around my bed like figures from a nightmare, bloodshot eyes looking down at me through the holes in their masks. I knew which one was my father because of the black and red ski mask he was wearing, the same one he'd worn to take me sledding when I was smaller.

They loaded me into the back of a van with the other boys, ten of us who'd all turned thirteen since last year, and drove off into the night. I didn't know what to expect. I'd heard the stories, of course, but they were all different. I think the men probably changed what happened every year. They wanted us to be prepared, but not complacent.

What happened next is hard to remember. Sometimes it feels like a dream, though I know it wasn't. I remember how cold it was, the long walk deep into the woods, the flashlights shining on the rocks and roots of trees below our feet. I can still hear the boys crying out for their fathers who stood apart in the shadows with their faces hidden. I remembered other things, too horrible, too unbelievable to be true. So that night was like a blind spot, a scar on my eye that I couldn't see past, although I could still sense things moving behind the haze if I looked long enough.

When Daniel turned twelve, he brought my old weights into his bedroom and started working out three times a day. I could hear the weights clink and thump on the floor above, sometimes deep into the night when they woke me up. I wanted to go upstairs and tell him to stop, that he needed his sleep. I wanted to tell him that he was wasting his time, that when the time came, none of this What would matter. But I figured that would only upset him, or he'd just ignore me. So I left him alone and learned to sleep through the clink and thump of the weights on the other side of the ceiling above.

As the months went by, I watched Daniel change himself. His arms and chest grew harder and stronger. That was not the only change. Years earlier, I'd watched my dying father go through a process of removing himself from the rest of us, a sort of deliberate cutting-off of his earthly mortal ties. In his final days, I realized that it wasn't that he couldn't recognize me—he was *willing* himself to not recognize me, to not care. And even though I know it was what he needed to face what was coming, it made me angry. I felt that same anger toward Daniel now. I loved him, but I didn't know how to love what he was becoming.

You always think you're going to have more time. Time for one more conversation, one more question, one more chance to pause and think and breathe. Even when you know there's not.

The week before Daniel's thirteenth birthday, I got a call from Monica. She was calling less and less lately, but I'd been expecting this one. Her voice was hard and accusatory.

"You're really going to let this happen?"

I felt the same tightening in my brain, too many thoughts jammed too close to move.

"I don't know..."

"What do you mean you don't know?"

"I mean...it's complicated..."

"It's not fucking complicated. Do you want your son to die? That's all there is to it. Do you want that?"

"No! Jesus, Monica, why would you even ask that?"

"Then *do* something."

She hung up, and I sat for a while, waiting for the blood pounding in my head to slow down. As the tangle of thoughts in my brain began to loosen themselves, one thought separated from the rest and slowly came into focus. We could just leave. Daniel and I. That was all we had to do. Just leave. The clarity of it stunned me.

That afternoon I went to the bank and withdrew fifteen hundred dollars. I would have taken all of it, but I didn't want it to look suspicious. It also would have meant that we were never coming back. I didn't want to think about that now, because I was afraid it might stop me.

I waited till dark before I asked Daniel to get in the car with me. When he asked where we were going, I told him I was taking him out for his birthday dinner. I was praying there was still just enough of the little boy left in him to go along with this. When he walked out to the car with me, I felt a rush of guilt and relief.

I dared a quick glance over at Daniel as we headed down Route 9. In profile, his face looked even leaner and harder than I'd realized it had become. His nose that had already been broken twice in martial arts class reminded me of a seasoned boxer or a Roman gladiator. When we started to get closer to the outskirts of town, I heard Daniel shift uneasily in his seat. "Where are we going, Dad?" he asked, and suddenly he was five years old again. My heart hurt so hard for a moment, I was afraid to say anything. I breathed deeply, swallowed, and said what I'd prepared to say.

"I thought we'd go on a little trip, buddy. You know, just you and me."

Daniel's reaction was immediate and harsh. He didn't have to see the suitcases I'd packed and hidden in the trunk, or all the cash I'd taken from our account and stashed in my wallet to know what was going on.

"Stop the car," he said, his voice cold and hard.

Tell him the truth, I thought. "Buddy…"

"Dad!" he shouted, "Stop the fucking car!"

Before I could say anything, Daniel reached across the seat and grabbed on to the steering wheel. I tried to pull it back and felt just how strong he was. The car veered wildly to the right. I stomped down on the brake, and we lurched to a halt, the front two wheels off the road. Before I could say anything, Daniel threw the door open, got out of the car and started walking back in the direction we'd come from. I called his name, but he kept walking, not looking back. That was when it hit me. *He wants this. He wants this to happen.*

Cursing under my breath, I threw the car into drive, made a U-turn and started after him. He must have known I was right behind him, but he kept walking and didn't turn around.

The sharp WHOOP of a police siren pierced my chest. I saw blue and red lights washing over Daniel, illuminating the inside of my car. I stopped and watched the police cruiser roll slowly past me on the left and pause alongside of Daniel.

When I opened the car door and started to get out, the officer turned and shouted, *"Sir....stay in your vehicle!"* I did as I was told. I watched as the officer talked with Daniel, then walked him back to our car. Daniel reluctantly climbed into the passenger seat, and the officer shut the door behind him.

At first I thought they might let us go home, just to prepare ourselves. But of course, we'd had thirteen years to do that. I knew that one more hour, one more day, even one more year wouldn't make any difference now. Like I said, you always think you're going to have more time.

We followed the police cruiser at a funereal pace, not too close, but not too far. On the way there, all the words I could have said but never had swelled up inside of my throat and died. Daniel didn't speak either. I risked a glance at him from the corner of my eye and saw him sitting straight with his chin held high, trying to make himself look bigger, older, stronger than he really was. It was a look I knew well, and it broke my heart.

Other cars came out to join us, and soon we were a procession, rolling through the darkened town. Lights flicked on in windows as we passed, hands pulled back curtains, and unseen eyes looked out. I wondered how many boys were watching us, how many mothers, how many fathers. What were they thinking? Were they picturing themselves in our place?

The last lights of town faded behind us and we drove for a while in pitch darkness. The police cruiser made a left turn off the road and we followed down a narrow gravel trail. When the cruiser's headlights illuminated a metal gate, chained and locked, we stopped while one of the cops got out to unlock it. In the glow of the headlights, I could see that he'd already put on his ski-mask. Then we were rolling forward again, tires rumbling over tree roots and ruts in the dirt. We paused for the last car to lock the gate behind us, then we were rolling forward again, deeper and deeper into the darkness.

And this is where an insane thought came to me, that maybe I was wrong about what I remembered. Maybe my father had never really beaten me and tied me to a tree. Maybe there had been no inhuman, ravening things trying to kill us. No real monsters. No dead boys. *Fathers don't do these things,* that's what I thought. Fathers don't lead their sons like cattle to be slaughtered. Fathers don't hand their sons over to monsters. Of course they don't. Not really. It was all just a tradition, some kind of game. I almost laughed with relief, but the sound that came out of my throat was more like a gasp or a sob. Daniel heard it and turned and looked at me. It was the first time that I saw him look afraid.

When we finally got to the place, it wasn't the way I remembered it. No bonfires casting flickering shadows, just the blinding glare of headlights from the police car and a few pickup trucks. The trees didn't look as tall or frightening as they once had, and seemed spaced further apart, like they were retreating from something. But the faces of the men, hidden in their cloth bandanas and black ski masks; those were the same.

One of the masked figures approached me and spoke in a harsh whisper. *"What the hell are you doing?"* I recognized Carl's voice. *"Here..."* he thrust a black ski-mask toward me. A few yards away, I saw one of the masked police officers turn and seem to stare at me. *"Put it on,"* Carl hissed. I hesitated. I wanted Daniel to be able to see my face.

"Put it on!" Carl hissed again. Slowly, with numb hands, I pulled the ski-mask over my head. It felt scratchy and tight over my face, and smelled like something that had been buried for a long time.

I looked around for Daniel and found him standing with a group of six other boys. They'd all taken off their shirts and stood huddled close together as if for warmth, their eyes closed and turned away from the blinding lights that made the rings in their chests glitter and shine.

Two men came forward holding a thick rope. I watched them pass the rope through the ring in the first boy's chest, then the next. When they got to the third boy, he made a frightened, sobbing sound and tried to back away, but one of the men held him by the arms until the rope had been passed through the ring in his chest. After that, he stood quietly, face turned downward as if the urge to flee had been drained out of him.

When they got to Daniel and were passing the rope through his ring, he held his head high and didn't move or make a sound. For a fleeting moment I felt proud of him, then a surge of panic and shame. There was nothing good about to happen here. Nothing to celebrate or be proud of. But instead of energizing me and moving me to act, the surge of shame left me drained and empty, unable to move or speak. I thought of the tree my father had tied me to, how weak and useless I'd felt.

Holding on to the rope, the men led the boys over to a large, heavy-looking metal plate on the ground, the kind that construction crews use to cover holes in the highway. A bulldozer rumbled into the light with another masked man at the controls, lowering its blade and pushing the heavy plate aside with a grating, sliding sound. That's when I heard them. The same sounds I heard in my nightmares for years, now rising up from that hole in the ground. Not human, not animal. Something in-between. It was true. It was all true.

Holding both ends of the rope, the men pulled the boys into a circle around the pit, then pulled the rope tighter until the boys were standing at the very edge. I could see Daniel still standing upright, his eyes looking straight ahead.

The sounds from the pit grew louder. Then the boys began to cry. One by one, their faces crumpled and twisted and grew shiny with tears in the harsh headlights. I could hear at least two of them crying out for their mothers. The men around me grew nervous and impatient, shuffling closer, lowing like cattle. Only Daniel made no sound, his face turned upward toward the light. I suddenly felt a surge of rage. Why didn't he get away when I gave him the chance? What was he trying to prove? Who did he think he was?

The horrible inhuman snarling from below grew louder. Claws scrambled and scraped at the sides of the pit. The other boys stopped crying and began screaming. What could I do? I had no weapon. No power to stop what was happening, no way to stop this thing that had been coming for years. It was stronger than I was. It had always been stronger.

That was when I saw Daniel reach up and take hold of the ring in his chest. He held it tightly in his fingers and pulled hard. I saw the skin on his chest stretch outward, farther and farther.

I want you to picture a boy tearing himself open and stepping outside of his own skin. Picture him growing taller and taller, his hair grown long and wild, fanning out like flames around his fierce snow-white face. Picture him rising taller than the trees, a long sword in his hands splitting the air like a whirlwind and laying waste to his enemies. If I told what I saw, would you think I was making it up, because the truth is too horrible to remember? Or would you realize that I was telling you something true, that I was seeing Daniel as he really was?

Could you do it? If it was the only thing left to do and you had no choice? Tear yourself open and step outside of the skin you were born in? You'd better start thinking about that. Because we always think there's going to be more time. Even when there's not.

JONATHAN GREENHAUSE

NON-SENTIENT THINGS

When alone, I start embracing hiking boots & doorknobs,
lampshades & test-tubes. I make out
with nail-files & fabric softeners, get high on products
from the US Postal Service, chart out future plans
with feminine hygiene pads
& vats of citronella repellent. My on-line psychologists
explain I resort to this because it's hard to open up
to people too quick to judge, to acquaintances who'd prefer
to alter how I think: A linoleum floor's rarely critical,
is predictably there whenever I lie down;
& straw is practical, too, as are backpacks, plastic cones,
& other things as well, how the road's dotted white line
keeps us oriented, is somehow acutely aware
of its limited function. I wind up in bed with bowling balls
& hatchback sedans, dream of a better world
with only me & these things, a honeymoon with my words
& their prolonged silences; yet my wife & sons
are notoriously missing. I imagine them criticizing me
for always living in this fabricated world
accompanied by nail-files & shoelaces, how all I hear
is the echo of disembodied thoughts impossible to share.

LESLEY HART GUNN

THE ROUNDING HOUR

We dared each other to go into the woods alone during the rounding hour, when the falling sun ignited the tops of the trees before dying. As that last burst of light yawned across the horizon, stretching the claw-like shadows of branches along the moldering ground below, we braved the whispery depths of the forest. Each of us took our turn, tying one end of a long, knotted ribbon to our wrists before breeching the thicket of trees that caught our hair and raked our skin. The ribbon kept us safely tethered to a root outside, to our predictable lives and controlled routine, while our steps carried us under the heavy canopy to witness the sounds of the nocturnal world waking to its dusky morning.

The contrast of the rounding hour made it all seem more exciting, darkness peppered with the last laughing cracks of sunlight. As the shafts of light grew thin, we held tightly to our tether and listened. Each snapping twig was a blood thirsty monster and each hoot or cackle a yellow eyed demon. Inside we remembered our mothers' warnings: *Where there are trees, there are wolves.* They wiped their knives in great slashes across their aprons, bleeding smiles cut perfectly across the white cloth, while our fathers' installed satellite dishes, attempting to distract us, to placate the pull of the woods and extinguish the wanderlust. We wanted more than their banal fears and prosaic lives so we ignored their warnings and left our manicured homes to force ourselves to witness the birth of night emerging from its mossy gestation. Creatures drowning in darkness danced deeper into the shadows. The damp air exhaled a chill across our clammy skin. We were afraid of what else we might see, but also hopeful that we would see something terrifying, something memorable. When the ribbon grew taut, we returned, pulling ourselves hand over hand along each knot, the menacing night dragging at our heels. When we burst into the last gasp of the sunset, breathless and relieved, we took the ribbons from our hair, adding another notch to our tether for next time, another step into the murky unknown.

* * *

When Merilee walked into the woods for the last time, we waited on the periphery, talking about things of little consequence, crushes at school or homework we'd lost. The shadows of the rounding hour died into night and Merilee still hadn't returned. We found the tether layered on the ground, coiled like a sleeping snake. We called her name and reeled the ribbons in, finding the end frayed and empty. We entered the woods together, one hand on the ribbon, the other reaching out into the shadows, dangling like worms on a single hook. The darkness bred hysteria and the no longer sleepy surroundings propagated fear with each hiss or rustle. Our eyes flooded with the indistinguishable weight of the night as the branches drew welts across our bodies. We pulled ourselves out of the thicket and back to our homes with cries of terror spilling from our mouths.

Parents took their lights and axes and lined up across the woods. Their flashlights held back the dark, illuminating all but Merilee. The calls of concern dotted the night air, keeping us buried in our shock filled blankets. They returned with regret etched into their faces. *She was taken by the rounding hour. Captured by trees and swallowed by shadows.* We felt ashamed as her parents cried into the same night we once found alluring. Our complicity in her disappearance burned scarlet across our cheeks. We wound up the ribbons and returned home, feeling guilty about the downy feathers cradling our heads. Merilee would have a pillow made of roots and dirt, or worse, a bed in the maw of some great unnamed beast.

* * *

We left things just inside the cover of trees, like small bits of bread, an apple or two, whatever we could sneak from the table, in case Merilee still wandered. The food disappeared, and we told ourselves that she wasn't gone; she weaved her way through the trees, keeping the secrets of the forest. We all had secrets, of course, but Merilee had been made of them. Before she disappeared, she disguised her secrets as irrational behavior or depression. She took off her shoes before entering the woods so she could show us the nicks and scratches left by the piney forest floor on the pale soles of her feet. She wandered alone late at night, knocking on our windows when we were sleeping, slipping inside to show us her bloody knees, begging us to ask what happened, to pull a string and watch her unravel. She crawled into our beds, pressing the chill of the night against our fevered skin. Her soft whimpering on our shoulders kept us awake as she drifted into a fitful sleep. We didn't know what questions to ask then, or how to help, but once she was gone we revealed what little we knew. We watched her parents unravel in her wake, every abuse and appetite uncovered as we finally found the words to make our accusations and to give Merilee back her voice. We brought blame to their door, hoping that if they were exposed, Merilee might come home.

It wasn't the Rounding Hour that took her; her parents drove her away. We tried the words on, looking for evidence in our memories, to force everything to make sense, to fall as neatly into place as our houses cut horizontally across the landscape, but Merilee did not come home and we began to doubt our assumptions. *If she made the choice to let go, couldn't she also choose to come back?* We preferred to think of her cutting herself loose, because the only other option was being ripped from us against her will. We wanted to believe in the Merilee that was wild and spontaneous, but that meant acknowledging that she made a choice to leave us, that maybe we were part of what she was running from. We made pacts to each other and cut our ribbon into pieces. We tied them around our wrists to prove our loyalty and acknowledge our failure, we screamed our love and apologies into the thicket of trees, but Merilee still didn't come home.

The ribbons followed us to the chapel where we sat in back pews and pondered our transgressions as the preacher pontificated about the dangers of the woods. We looked to the window, where the trees tapped their fingers along a stained-glass impression of Saint Sebastien. As the rounding sun spilled his red arrow wound across the dusty floor, we fingered the knots of our grimy ribbons and thought about feeling the moss between our toes, the brush of a leaf across our cheeks, or the gouge of a pinecone in the soft arch of a foot. There was an ache that cried to be satiated, a lure of the trees that a simple knot of silk could not satisfy.

* * *

The following years created new complications. Changing bodies brought unwanted attention and the trauma of adolescence. *Merilee is lucky she won't ever have to deal with this.* The idea of either a dead or aging Merilee settled over us, as suffocating as the woods themselves. It was more comfortable to imagine her in her pre-adolescent form, wandering the woods in the carelessness of a never-ending childhood. The possibility of having to mature and age while also being lost was too cruel. We grew to hate our bodies and envy hers. We painted our faces and pierced our ears. We stopped leaving food inside the trees. As the magic of childhood gave way to the realities of adulthood, our perspectives shifted. There were no more flashlights and ribbons, no bare foot walks or hidden demons. If a passing branch caught our hair or clothes, we brushed it off. We got devices of distraction and crowded around the screens, our eyes wide with the glare of a shadow-less world. We typed Merilee's name into search engines and found numerous forums and support groups for missing people. We tweeted and blogged, regurgitating all our pain onto sites engineered to handle our maturing grief. Strangers responded with tear stained emojis and praying hands.

* * *

Through the years there were sightings, flashes of a small girl, sticks in her hands and a long, frayed ribbon trailing from her hair. Images of homeless people and runaways were posted in our chat rooms. *This is not our Merilee. She is lost, not deranged.* We posted our well-reasoned assertions, receiving responses that both supported and countered, and we responded to the responses, moving deeper into the darkening world of artificial arguments with disembodied voices. Some claimed there were too many Merilee's, some called us liars. *If so many were lost, the woods would be full of screams and footprints.* They didn't know the forest muted voices, like a clammy hand across the mouth. Hate threads wound themselves around us like new barbarous ribbons, and we barely remembered the time when excitement meant taking a step into the trees and daring the night to crash over us.

* * *

Discrepancies eventually grew in our memories. Was she gentle and energetic, or sullen and withdrawn? Was it her mother she hated more, or her father? Did we hear someone crying when we walked into the woods? Our recollections grew thin and flimsy, subject to suggestion. Eventually we couldn't remember what parts of Merilee were real or imagined. We tried to reassemble her character in blog posts but kept imposing our own ordeals and inadequacies on her until she was little more than the shell for our collective distresses. Our fears and secrets turned her into the wildling of the forest, still roaming through the mystery of forgotten hopes and repressed secrets, waiting for someone to find her and bring her home.

Eventually we pretended it never happened. Merilee was the name of a girl in someone else's dream. The hate threads slowly came lose, as ill-fitting as our discolored ribbons shoved into piles under our beds. Instead we overshared the least interesting parts of ourselves: pictures of parties, food and drinks, people we would forget about and sentiments drowning in hashtags. The unknown was now some other life in pictures, some Instagrammed pseudo-world that was perfectly lit and full of contingent philosophies and altruisms. Our devices flashed with mechanized tweets and sculpted communications even as we slept. The woods were little more than the barrier that kept us from the city. Our ears filled with the pumping sounds of urban life. The flashing lights of a club never left any beckoning shadows and we never dreamed of taking off our shoes to feel the dirty crust of concrete and litter under our feet. Merilee fluttered through our minds only after too many drinks, remaining buried under the simulacrum of the urban forest. She was gone by the time we rubbed the sleep from our eyes, leaving our sense of wonder to rot alongside the city stench.

* * *

When the myth of Merilee came back to us through our children, bringing old stories to the surface like a decayed and bloated figure from a body of water, we told them there was nothing to fear. We dressed them in new ribbons and histories, claiming the witch of the woods was lost and alone, and the best thing to do if one was lucky enough to see her, was to tell her to come home. There were no longer woods in our backyards, but the sprawl of an insatiable city. The soft, decaying ground stretched into cement roads and broken sidewalks. The bark and leaves of trees became brick and mortar high-rises, persistently reaching for the sky and glittering with glass from root to stem. From the shadows came traffic and pedestrians, phones in their hands, screens flooding their faces in a moon-like glow. Perhaps this was always how it was, concrete and metal posing as nature, giving the appearance of growth when only decay was possible.

After seasons of forgetfulness we began to see it again, to remember the rounding hour as it curved the shadows of the buildings around the sidewalks and alleyways. The newly planted trees sparkled and struggled to take root in the final gasp of every dying day. Our memories were reborn through the eyes of experience, our bodies reincarnated as our mothers. *Where there are trees, there are wolves.* We hoped to kill the allure of the rounding hour we knew would come for our children, but soon learned, as our parents did, that some battles are meant to be fought but not won.

As age and experience pooled around us, we searched for Merilee again. We looked for the warnings in every passing face, the red rimmed eyes, the bare feet and sullen smiles. We left the occasional loaf of bread on the curb, hoping it would go missing. We saw her turning a corner, running in the distance, a flash of dark hair and ribbons drawing us on, just one step further into our re-emerging memories. She appeared in what was left of the woods, sidewalks splintered by grass, rotting leaves, and the occasional sparrow on an anemic urban branch. We wanted to catch her, to untangle the twigs from her hair, scrub the dirt from her nails and put Band-aids on her knees, then we'd tell her the rounding hour couldn't hold her anymore, if she'd just come out of the darkness, if she'd just come back to us.

When the sun started its descent, and the shadows crawled across the busy streets, we stuffed our phones into our pockets, took off our shoes, and tied the ribbons around our wrists. No longer afraid of getting lost or being taken, we weaved our way through the buildings and trees, our hands outstretched, our steps deliberate, our mouths tirelessly calling into the darkness, beckoning the lost girl home.

REBECCA LILLY

TESTAMENT

"Nothing's by chance," said Mr. Ellis, the gravedigger then, reaching out for some flowers and shaking them. "No one these days speaks to the dead, but the dead get around." He stepped out of a hole, shaking off soil.

"Flowers *always* mean another death to think about," he remarked, *apropos*. I wouldn't have asked him to lunch, but he was good company those hours I sat, jotting notes for poems.

That night, on a gravestone, he left a photo of me sitting on the iron fence. His way of saying, *Go home.* White-ghosted with flash, taken at night on the sly as I stared at the slabs.

I am a ghost at times, my eyes lighting flowers through the spiked, lattice fence, searching hard for signs of life, proof I haven't vanished yet. (I was there every night for meditation, imagining a flower in my head. *Save the day,* the sky in my eyes kept saying.)

Mr. Ellis refers to my poetry as *my remains*, and asks for a line or two as testament to sanity.

"Brace yourself. Here it is: *At the foot of a hill, a dark and stormy wind.*"

"I get it," he brushed off his dirt-caked shirt, eyes narrowed to slits. "*You're* the dark and I'm the stormy wind."

"It isn't finished," I shrugged. Not that I *wouldn't* be inclined to this. I considered it a moment, staring at the page, then put him in the poem:

As the gravedigger shovels, he descends into his hole, where dark extinguishes the casts and edges of every shadow.

Perhaps his disappearance will be inspirational.

JULIA LILLARD

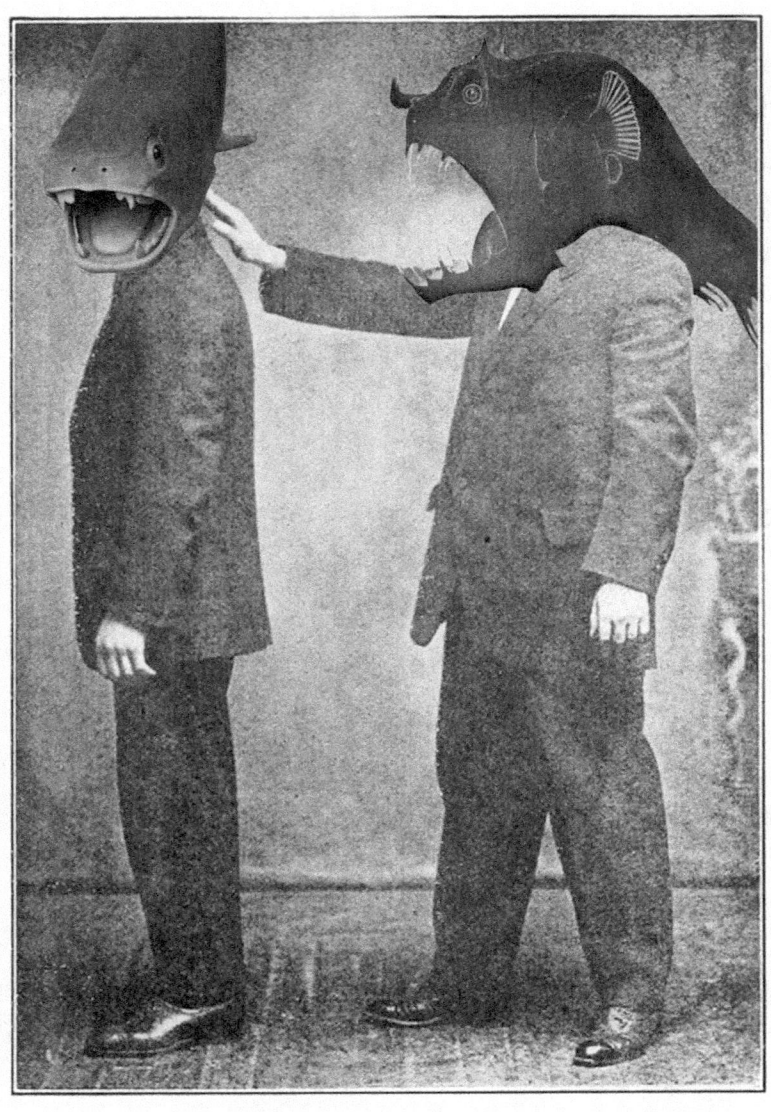

something dark

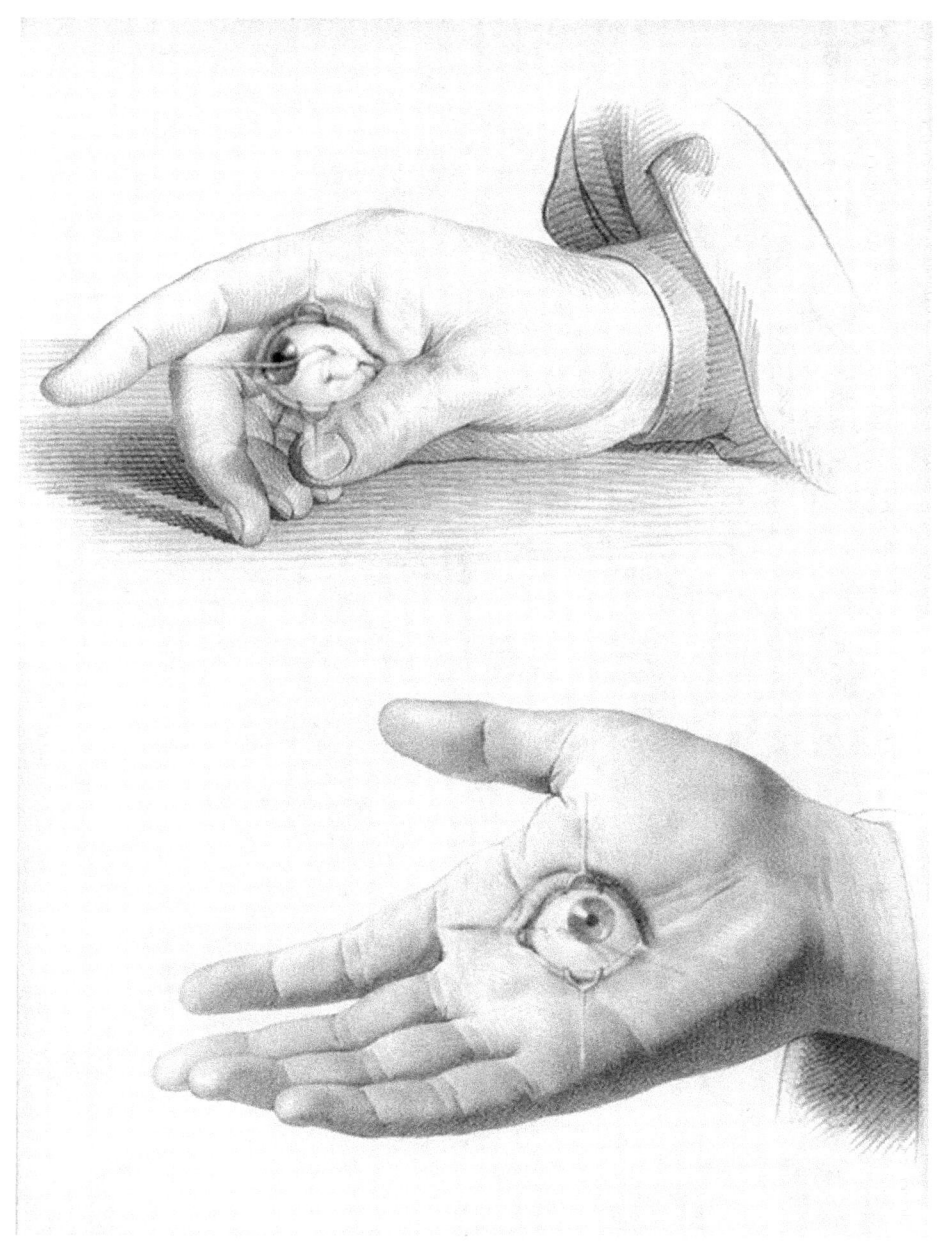

it can't hurt

something worth saving

THE FOX AND THE MIGUELS

The only fox in town was not a real one, but the former Music Television Supervisor who after too many instances of working the name Miguel into every episode possible was commanded to enter the fusion transmogrifier and repeat the code "I can't believe what I've done" for his given sentence. He'd remain a fox for the better part of the week and still expected to do his job, which for a fox was difficult. Not because he couldn't reach any equipment or the conference table or take any calls, but because something itched in him to dart away from the building towards that thing he should have never ever bothered with in the first place.

While eyeing reports for the week, he could hear a little too much farther into the hall and therefore past the work lounge and Barbara Ann's mousesqueak of a voice that came from her own transgression and stayed with her well beyond. The word in and down the hall was that Miguel was some sort of young lover or ex-lover or jilted lover or stalked lover or dreamed lover or obsessed *or* obsessed over lover. The word was that Fox had a head full of Miguel for one loverly reason or another and that his only way of reaching him was through the at-first-subtle-until-not-so-much name-drops in lyrics and eventually artists named Miguel.

The kicker came when thinking he had been too obvious, Fox had found songs and musicians about and within the city of San Miguel de Allende and insisted on their use throughout all of the final arc of season 7. Complaints came in that a music syndicate in San Miguel de Allende had their claws in Fox and that he were a mere puppet. Fearing any retribution on the Mexican city or Mexican Americans within the town, Corporate conducted an investigation on Fox and the consistent uses of Miguel, which concluded in never quite being sure what was going on.

Thus, the "I can't believe what I've done" code was chosen over the more severe commands "Can you ever forgive me?" and "I don't deserve what I have."

At least, Fox said to himself over and over for comfort and grounding, *I'm not a potato or car tire*. The sentence of transmogrification for more severe crimes often resulted in edible or inanimate objects that were sure to be consumed, used, thrown out, set on fire, and/or simply forgotten in a field only for the punished to suffer a life-threatening exposure to the elements. And while some were careful to inspect vegetables and tires left on sidewalks and fields, others were not. The tale of a woman POOFing back into her human body while having been "t-mogged" (as the kids say) into the rear right rim of a mint green 1976 Pontiac GTO to be squished and splatted all over the road as well as the hot ass car was one that even the youngest citizen of the town knew. Particularly when they wouldn't finish their dinner or put away their toys.

Fox tried to shake off the fear of being mistaken for a regular fox by remembering, first, there weren't in any town to begin with (which should be an indication of his once-humanness), and, second, Fox could start fires with its tail, which was a pretty cool thing to be able to do. In fact, the starting of fires was so incredibly tempting that sometimes Fox would pretend he had to get to a meeting very, very quickly and race down the hall allowing his tail to trail against the wall and subsequently a great amount of singeing and smoldering lines appeared each day down the hallway. Some worried that much like Barbara Ann's mouse squeak voice, the foxfires would be something all would have to live with for the rest of Fox's short life.

Fox's unexpected death could likely be traced to not just his crime of all-things-Miguel, but even before that when Miguel was a name strewn throughout his text messages from a slew of spam. Though he never knew who Miguel was, Fox received messages for Miguel daily for some weeks. The messages always came from different numbers so he couldn't properly block any of them, and none were elaborate enough to give him any sense of who Miguel might actually be. Fox had only to start visiting every Miguel in town, watching through their windows in his new stealthy fox way and looking for some sort of clue that said "Yes, this is Miguel. Yes, you have all his messages."

The messages always ended with something about debt-relief, but it was the beginning of each that eventually got to Fox and his overwhelming care for Miguel and his well-being. "We know things can be tough, Miguel, please give us a call." "Miguel, you are running out of time. We can help." "With only a few days left before the next credit rating, please know we are here if you need us, Miguel." And finally: "I'm within reach, Miguel. Please return our call to talk about lowering your federal tax debt, Miguel." It was that second instance of the name that really got to Fox. Sure it could have been a mistake, a glitch in the automated text service's algorithm. But Fox had drank an entire bottle of wine by himself in the first 45 minutes of being home one evening when the text came and in that moment, the only thing that filled his then-human heart was poor Miguel drowning in debt with no ability to reach out to those standing by ready to save him.

Miguel was a man stuck in quicksand. He was digging a hole and couldn't see the edges of earth ready to crash down on him. Miguel was walking on a cliff ledge and didn't know he was on the lip of the canyon and there was no, not a single, not even one bit of rock or ground supporting that lippy edge. Miguel's sleeve was close to knocking over a glass of wine that would end up starting an electrical fire that would burn him to a crisp. Miguel's foot was about ready to hit a crack in the cement. Miguel was looking at his car radio when he should have been watching the street. He didn't check both ways. Above Miguel was a piano hoisted up and up by rope to a fourth story window and the rope was fraying after a small bitch of a bird landed on it and pulled free a bit of thread for a nest and the piano was teetering and even though the men hoisting it were saying "Whoa whoa whoa" and one even managed a "look out"—Miguel had his airpods in and was ready to meet whatever could possibly exist between the hard thud of a now cracked open piano and the equally cracked cement below.

Miguel Miguel Miguel! Fox's late nights tossing and turning took their toll. And after countless tries to ring back any of the numbers and only getting more automated messages, most of which asked for Miguel's Social Security Number or astrological sign, Fox knew he had to do something. Had to reach for Miguel in one way or another. It was his duty and, to be honest, he was a little miffed that the transmogrifier did not turn him into a guard dog or grand elk. Fox used what tools came easily to him: his authority and music, which he paid a price for but to no avail. Or so he thought. While watching a particularly lonely Miguel make himself some Spaghetti O's—a Miguel that also looked at a bill in the mail and hung his head before throwing it into the recycling pile—Fox had a twitch in him that screamed to Miguel that he was not alone. And the more Fox felt out his twitch and really tried to embrace his own Foxness (but not too much because it was also true that some never came back from their sentence when going full paintbrush or salamander or rambutan), the more Fox realized he was not just not alone but he was *very much* not alone.

Just beyond him a group of people had begun to gather. And among them he could hear some muttering, one word over and over and said in the sides of the mouth or just along a trembling lip. Miguel. Miguel. Miguel. However it was that the group had come to this particular Miguel and not any of the many others, Fox would never know. It was quite possible they had followed him, quite possible that somewhere within the myriad of Miguel songs and that one mention he snuck into the background of a track, the viewers had been following him for some distance and from Miguel to Miguel. Or it could simply be that this particular Miguel was well-known for owning the best sandwich shop in town named Miguel's. No matter the reason, the group was now a crowd and nearly a mob. MiguelMiguelMiguel, the muttering became a chant and it was in this moment that Fox's ability to decipher chronology and cause/effect slid down its own embankment and Fox was very entirely certain that he was there to save Miguel and that the messages he received led him to this very moment to keep Miguel safe from the angry mob—if it was indeed angry because for the most part they just seemed eager and hungry for a look at Miguel.

What Fox did next no one will ever forgive even though on occasion a person or two will try to understand where Fox was coming from and one or two would tweet about it with a "hot take" or "I don't know who needs to hear this" and someone would write an essay for the latest trend site flashing expanded hot takes and I don't know who needs to hear this articles. The latest theory on Fox would catch fire, much as the angry mob had (by then Fox had decided they were indeed angry and he was left with one recourse).

Fox was just a blur of red as he raced and raced around the crowd, his tail catching sparks on the ground around them and on occasion the pant leg of a person or two until the sparks were bright and often enough that the very weeds and cloth around them did not cower in the heat or flame and it was almost an invitation to come alight. Fox nearly died himself when he once or twice figured eighted through the crowd, just hoping to end the screams a little earlier since the people in the middle of the crowd had yet to catch fire and only saw smoke and the crushing of the bodies around them.

"For Miguel!" the Fox cried and believed it. So much so that when placed in front of the courts to account for his crime, now murderer, he said it again and watched as his sloth lawyer began the first slight shoulder tremble that eventually became a big shrug-sigh long after the rest of the courts had left. They had very nearly been ready to acquit as this wasn't the first time animal transmogrify backfired when one creature or another acted in just the ways they always expected to, their animal instinct taking over. They had very nearly let Fox go because they did understand why a mob outside of Miguel's home would have in fact been dangerous to Miguel and those in the vicinity and why a fox would (out of instinctual fear for itself) respond in self-preservation. But Fox didn't fear for itself, but for Miguel and in insisting that was indeed his reasoning, Fox proved himself still too human to get by on the Beast Will Be Beast clause.

When rustling Fox into the transmogrifier again for his new crime, which wasn't in fact called murder, but rather a type of obsession, a code could not be decided upon soon enough and now in the machine already and before he could stop himself, Fox reflecting on how much he ruined his own defense let alone his entire life on the spam texting, he muttered "I can't believe I said what I said" and poof, he was made into a toaster, one that found itself thrown into the tub of and with an entirely different Miguel who was told by all his friends way too many times that *No, no. The television was not, in fact, trying to reach you, Miguel.*

 RAY KEIFETZ

SALT POINT

Last night
I heard a splash,
an oar
pulling through the shallows,
your voice
Marry
before the water turns you white,
a ghost takes your hand—

Gulls fly through the spray
already dry.
A lone boat sails out
already stove.
I was taken
long before you warned me.
I turned white the first tide.

If you ever reach the shore,
look for me,
come to me,
lie down beside me.
Cover us snug
with kelp and flies;
we have forever
to dissolve.

 JOHN POSPICHAL

THE MARIONETTES

Somewhere in the cold heights of the Caucasus, far away from human civilization, there is a dark and mysterious forest. In the middle of this forest is a clearing where no tree ever grows, and no cloud passes over. Here, in a little village, live the marionettes.

The marionettes are puppets. Each one is attached to a bunch of strings that leads straight into the sky. Their hands have strings attached, their arms have strings attached, and their legs, their feet, and their heads have strings attached. Even their lips are strung up.

But for all that, the marionettes live very normal lives—just like yours and mine. They sleep, they work, and they play. They get married, have children, grow old, and die.

And although they are made of wood—and when they eat the food just falls out of their mouths, all chewed up, back onto their plates, and when they make love they just touch their wooden lips and bump their wooden bodies together, and when they give birth their children just float down into their arms from the clear blue sky, and when they die their bodies just rise up and disappear—none of this bothers them. To the marionettes, it is all quite normal and good.

But everything was put into question one day, long ago, when a little boy entered their village, a boy made of flesh and blood. How did it happen? Where did he come from? Nobody knew. He just walked out of the forest one afternoon, and looked around.

The first marionette who saw him was a little girl named Maddy. She was gathering sticks by the forest's edge when he appeared. Suddenly she straightened, and clutched the bundle of sticks to her chest.

"Hello," said the boy, staring at her.

"Hello," said Maddy, staring back.

But then the boy saw the other marionettes. And the other marionettes saw him. Everyone in the village stopped what they were doing and stared at the boy, whose mouth began to form into a little grin.

"Why, you're all made of wood!" he declared.

At this the marionettes were highly displeased. They looked down at themselves and then at the boy, and their wooden bodies rattled with rage.

"Arrest him!" cried one of the elders of the village, and several of the marionettes sprang into action. The boy tried to run, but his pursuers, bounding and leaping through the air on their strings, captured him with ease. They dragged the boy kicking and screaming into the largest hut in the village. There they set him down before the elders and all the villagers.

Slowly, the little boy got to his feet, sniffling. He looked up and saw that the hut had no roof. He looked around and saw that all the marionettes were attached to strings.

"You're puppets!" he exclaimed.

"Silence!" thundered the elders, and the marionettes that guarded the boy struck him with wooden rods. The boy fell to his hands and knees, wailing and crying from the blows.

"Where have you come from?" an elder demanded in a harsh voice, his lips clapping loudly as he spoke.

"From my house," moaned the boy, in tears.

"Where is this house?" growled the elder.

"Through the woods," said the boy.

At this, the elders turned with creaking necks and looked at each other.

"Why have you come here?" another one asked.

"I didn't mean to," said the boy in a piteous tone. "I got lost."

The elders didn't respond. For a long time they murmured amongst themselves. Finally, with a loud command, they dismissed the onlookers, who slowly left the hut and returned to their homes. Then they turned to the boy with narrowed eyes.

"You are a devil!" proclaimed one.

"You have come here to hurt us!" declared another.

"You must be put to death!" pronounced a third.

The boy began to cry again. "I'm not a devil," he sobbed. "I just want to go home. Please, I'll never come back again. ...I promise!"

But the elders did not listen. They ordered the guards to lay the boy upon a table. Ropes were tied to his hands and feet and pulled taut. Then one of the guards picked up a knife.

When the boy saw the knife, he screamed and begged for mercy. But the marionettes ignored him. The guard with the knife bent over the boy's body, pinched a bit of his belly with one hand and leveled the knife with the other. But just as he was about to pierce the boy's flesh, a voice called down from above.

"Stop!" said the voice.

Everyone turned. From a tree overlooking the hut, straddling one of the branches, a marionette looked down on them. It was Maddy.

"Don't hurt him!" she cried. "He's not a devil! He's not!"

The elders cursed angrily and ordered the guards to take her away. As they rushed outside, Maddy saw the little boy twist and turn upon the table, struggling to look up into the tree. Finally, with a great burst of effort he threw back his head, locked his eyes with hers, and everything else ceased to exist.

But then the guards grabbed her, pulled her down from the tree and carried her home to her parents. There she was whipped for spying on the elders, and locked in her room.

As she lay in bed that night, Maddy heard screaming in the distance. For a long time the screaming continued, and she cried all night for the little boy.

The next morning, the boy's skin was hanging from a little wooden cross outside the main hut.

The boy was the work of a sorcerer, the marionettes were told, sent there to destroy them. But the elders removed the magic from his body before it could harm the village.

The marionettes accepted this explanation and went on with their lives. Soon the skin was taken down and stored in a hut, and everyone forgot all about the little boy.

Everyone, that is, except Maddy.

Maddy thought about the boy day and night. She remembered the way he had said hello to her outside the forest. She remembered the way he had looked up at her in the tree. And she remembered the feeling she had felt then, a feeling she had never felt before. A feeling of complete emptiness.

One evening, Maddy crept into the hut where the boy's skin was stored and stole it. She brought the skin to her room and hung it carefully in the corner.

"You are not hard and rough like us, little boy," she whispered to the eyeless face. "You are soft and smooth."

She touched the skin and then touched her hard, wooden body. She raised the boy's arm and then released it. It dropped limply.

She raised her own arm, studied it, and let it drop. Then she moved the boy's mouth with her hand.

"I don't live here," she made the mouth say. "I got lost."

She put her hand to her own mouth. "I got lost," she said again. "I don't live here."

She moved her hand towards her mouth until it touched the string attached to her lips. With a start, she jerked it away.

Then she held up her hands. For the first time, she saw the strings. She saw them move when she moved her arms, and she saw how they rose, straight and taut, from every part of her. She looked up and followed them with her eyes until they disappeared among the stars. Then she gasped and sat down on the bed.

Slowly, she raised her hand again. It trembled in the starlight. With her other hand she pushed on the string attached to it. It moved in response. A cry escaped her lips, and she collapsed onto the bed. For a long time she lay there, staring at the stars.

In the middle of the night, she rose from the bed and went to her dresser. Opening a drawer, she removed a pair of scissors. Then, facing the mirror, she held up her hand, took a deep breath, and cut the string attached to it.

The hand hung limply, like the little boy's. She glanced at his skin in the corner of the room, so pale in the starlight. Then she cut the string to her forearm, and it also hung limply.

She continued to snip away the strings attached to her, going up and down one side and then starting on the other, cutting dozens, hundreds of strings.

Soon she had reduced herself to a jumbled pile of wood on the floor. Only a single string remained: the one attached to the hand which held the scissors. But no matter how hard Maddy tried, she could not cut it. She could not cut the final string.

The sky began to lighten. The door opened and Maddy's mother appeared. She saw the skin of the boy and the remains of her daughter, and she screamed in horror.

Then Maddy's father entered, and he shouted in despair. He went to his daughter, took the scissors from her hand and picked her up. As his wife wept and wailed on the floor, her body clattering as she heaved, he carried the girl outside.

With slow, plodding feet he walked through the village with the bundle of wood. Awakened by the cries and commotion, the villagers stood outside their homes and watched him pass by in the gray light.

Her father carried Maddy into the forest surrounding the village. Deeper and deeper he carried her, his strings cutting through the branches and leaves above. He continued until he reached a small clearing where a pit had been dug in the earth. There he fell on his knees and raised the remains of his daughter to the sky.

"Oh Gods," he cried. "Take this child away from us! Purge her memory from our souls! Cleanse us of this evil, we beg of you!"

Then he dumped the bundle of wood into the pit, and rushed away.

For a long time Maddy lay there, her hand still twitching and jerking, searching for the scissors that had been taken from it.

Eventually a shaft of moonlight pierced the trees above the clearing. It fell upon the ground and crept towards the pit. When it entered, Maddy's hand rose toward it like a charmed snake. Her arm followed, and then her trunk, and all her limbs.

On a single string she rose from the pit, through the branches and the leaves, higher and higher into the moonlit sky, until she disappeared.

In the village, the marionettes held a great festival. There was drumming and dancing, laughing and feasting. At the climax of the evening, the boy's skin was thrown into the fire, which caused it to flare up magnificently. At this, the marionettes cheered so loudly their strings vibrated all the way to the heavens, and a strange but harmonious music could be heard for miles around.

BRUCE MCALLISTER

THE BLEEDING CHILD TAROT

That is what the deck is called, and why I bought it at the little shop on the East Side last week. I look for him—the Bleeding Child—in these cards every night because the booklet says he is there if you will only look, and, if you find him, you'll have again what you have lost. I have lost so much.

But where is he?

Not in this card—in the wands, which are saplings, three of them in the night, their small blossoms white, not scarlet, though the earth they grow from in the darkness is the color blood might be inside us without light. Black heart, black blood moving through black vessels. The darkness of stone, of eternal sleep, of eyes that go out like the only stars in an evening sky. Can innocence and hope survive what has no light itself?

Or here. Two swords, their blades white, cross while a narrow white banner waves in a wind. The moon is above them, white too, but if I close my eyes, place my thumbs against them and press, the moon turns red in memory. Is every moon of childhood shared by brothers long ago a blood moon?

The King of Wands is a wolf with a thin branch in its jaws—torn from a tree we cannot see—floating in an evening sky that twinkles like a child's dream above it. It bears no blood on its lips or teeth or flank, or even, in its own dream, in its eyes, from the hunger there. It must wait patiently for blood, for a child to stumble, to fall to rocks so much like jaws.

The Nine of Wands. They are crossed. They are sticks, not branches with blooms, four laid against four and the ninth vertical, holding them up, a flame above them. A torch that says, *Do not despair.* A fire that says, *Whatever bleeds will not stop because of fire.* The crossed wands make a cross, but there is no body on that cross to bleed. The wands float in a storm-wracked sky, the silhouette of ragged mountains in the distance to frame, to give the fire meaning even without blood. An old voice—my own, trying to help me when the ghost of the boy I remembered kept whispering to me about blood—says, *Sometimes the light shines brightest against the darkness.* What felt like a lie then feels truer now.

The raven is headless. Or is it hiding its head in its wings? The seven swords do not pierce it. The claws are open and rigid, as if paralyzed by an eternity of seizing the dead. I look for a drop of blood anywhere, but there is none. The tips of the seven swords promise that someday each will have a drop, but that is someday. I must wait, the swords say. I must now have a patience with death that I have never shown and never will unless I raise my head from these dark feathers and soften my claws into gentle hands with those I love.

This is the Hierophant, and yet it is also an elk, huge, staring at us against the same starry, evening sky, a key—an actual key—to its right, hovering in the air—and another key to its left. What does the Hierophant wait for? Does it wait, as I do, to find the blood of the Bleeding Child wherever I might find it, where any of us might? Or is it waiting to understand the viewer, to understand why I might look for blood when there isn't any in this card, when life itself certainly must have many faces that are not bloody. The Hierophant's eyes, however, are black as tar. If only they glowed and glowed red, just a little, like our father's when he was drunk, I could have faith in finding the Child, in understanding why he bleeds.

The Lovers now. Two white cranes, dancing before us, could blind each other so easily and yet do not. Their vulnerable necks move in an easy love and careful ritual. In the tiny head of each crane is a particle of fear, and in that fear one of its eyes bleeds forever. But that is only a part of it, and not the most important. The great bodies dance on, and the particle is but illusion. Is this what the Bleeding Child is? A fear, a dream, a lie? Or is this—this very question—the lie, evil trying to make the Bleeding Child unimportant when everything depends on him, always has and always will, in a world that must live on like any other?

For a moment, in this one, the two flowers—Temperance—look familiar. I've seen flowers before that have blood on them. The blood of someone's Christ. *The Dogwood.* The petals make a cross, each petal with its hook, a fang, a talon, a little finger touched by blood. But these two flowers are not Dogwood, and the red spots on them are but pollen at the end of a stamen. Yet is the Child's blood not like this, a dust to be borne on the wind, on legs and wings, so that something important, once lost, can be saved?

Nor this one. These pentagrams—the pentacles—float above the snowy limbs and trunks of a tree that would be dead were there no snow, but that is, we know, sleeping, like the snake, dead but alive, coiled within it. Is its sap, which barely moves in the spring, full of iron, red too, or is it a blood we can never understand? Is the snow of its limbs and the silent earth around it a false holiness, a mask of purity that hides the inevitable decay of bodies, for it is dying, too, as all trees must? Would a hint of red blood help us understand that the Child, unlike the things of this world, bleeds forever in our memories and cannot die, though the grinning face I remember did and always will. As I watch, the center of each pentagram fills with scarlet and the color turns the snow below it the faintest pink, as if to say, *I am always here. I cannot die even though you think I am gone.*

The barn owl, an animal I have always loved—because it was there in the night by voice or flash of white wherever I played as a child and still is, whether I am trying to remember my brother, or trying to forget myself—flies toward me against the blackness of the night. Its eyes are holes through which I must see the night behind it, as if the owl were saying, *You believe I am here to fly at you, to make you think only of me, and yet what truly matters is what lies behind us all, the night of it, the darkness against which your brightness, like mine, though you do not believe it, can shine in the briefest moments of this life.* Its talons hold a scroll of white paper, a message, a ban, a holy text, but it does not offer it. The owl simply carries it through the night, and I have glimpsed them both in an instant of this life—bird and paper. As I do, I see the blood in this picture. It is in the tiny red flowers I can now see at the bottom of this card, drawn in a boy's jerky hand, because I am longer blinded by the white bird.

For a moment, I think I have found the Bleeding Child. It is the Devil Card, a human body, chained, face hidden by the long hair and an arm. But it isn't a child, an infant, a boy, and there is no blood. Why the Devil is chained, in pain, I do not know and never will, unless it is true, what people say—that a demon is but an unloved angel, or at least in his self-pity and rage at God believes he is. Or perhaps I am to see the Child in the chained man here. But why is there no blood? Do his chains hide his bleeding? A single pentacle floats above the man's head, but this does not matter. I understand and yet do not, but this mystery, too, does not matter—any more than the reason I smell our father's drunken breath in every breath I take, the violence of his hands, world without end.

I cannot find the Bleeding Child in these cards, though the booklet says I will. It is as if one card, perfect in every way, were missing, or it is there but I cannot see it because I look only for blood. I see blood that might be his, but I cannot see his body, the one—infant or boy—that has (the booklet tells me) been bleeding for two thousand years, the mistake he was that night long ago, a birth that shouldn't have been, under desert stars and to a darker Father, and so he bleeds forever for us, crying in the night, asking to be saved.

I turn one more card. The Magician is a butterfly—one I remember from childhood playing with my dark-haired, laughing brother near our school, in the field, among the saplings at forest's edge, in the twilight, the raven and the owl circling over us somewhere, below a blood-red moon. The butterfly has two great mock eyes on its lower wings, and each of the minor arcana below those wings. Wand, pentacle, sword, chalice. As I look, the eyes blink and begin to bleed just as my brother's did, stumbling on the path, falling to the rocks below because he was younger and clumsier and more frightened as we ran from our father dead drunk and sleeping deaf on the sofa at the house, from the fire we set beginning at the curtains and blossoming into bright red flowers, no movement in the body when I reached him except the blood on his head, which moved down to his eyes, covering them, to his cheeks and mouth, which opened just once. The butterfly closes its wings, opens them again. My brother blinks, his face healed, the blood gone, the taste of it on my lips now because, like a wolf standing over its elk, I lick it clean again and again. At the corner of his eyes, no longer bloody, is the old laughter, which I hear.

This is the Child.

 JACOB CHAPMAN

TWO POEMS

JUST LIKE EVERYONE ELSE

The motorcade sped by and startled me.
Loud motorcycles led the way,
followed by limousines with little flags
on their front corners. I didn't recognize
the flags or the man standing up
through the sunroof of the last limousine.
He blew kisses to the crowd
and kept yelling *Yes! Yes! Yes!*
No one else seemed to recognize him either,
but some people returned his kisses
and yelled *Yes!* anyway.
I turned to my unauthorized biographer,
who follows me everywhere,
and said *why don't you write a book about him?*
He shook his head and didn't say anything.
He's tracked down pretty much everyone
I've ever known and asked them
all sorts of questions about me.
I've told him multiple times
that he's following the wrong person,
that there's no great deed in my future.
That's not why I follow you, he told me once.
Why do you follow me? I asked.
If I told you, it would ruin everything, he said.
You'll have to wait and see,
just like everyone else.

THE SEAGULLS

When the seagulls arrived
after flying across a hundred miles of land,
I kept waiting for the sky to explode
or the earth to crack open.
The birds were everywhere,
and they seemed very calm
as they rested in the trees.
Someone tried to light the town on fire.
People started making public displays
of penance and self-flagellation.
Other people were constantly yelling
at each other, and groups would merge
and splinter. The weather was fine.
Our friends on the coast
asked about the seagulls,
but their days were peaceful.
Someone convinced half our town,
including me, to wear bird masks
that fit over our heads
whenever we went outside.
The eyeholes were big circles.
The faces and the beaks were white,
and the hoods were black.
The seagulls came out of the trees
and climbed all over our bodies.
That lasted for a few days, and then
they flew back to the coast.
We put our masks away
and returned to our lives.

No one ever talks about it.
Any of it. Whenever I try to bring it up,
people quickly change the subject.
Except my sister. We can talk about it,
and she knows it's always on my mind.
It's one of those things
that just happened, a square peg
in the round hole of the world.

 JOHN LEWIS

DINNER WITH [RUIN]

[<u>1936</u>: farmer struggles in the rain. Night: lightning
flickers like shutter bulbs from a movie premiere. Hail
is destroying his crops. Farmer's clothes: disheveled,
drenched, too large for his long, gaunt body. Pathetic hat]
[Rear: small homestead]
[Front and left: fields of wheat, sorghum, hay. A well. A
pigpen, chicken coop]
[Right: barn and pen enclosure, tractor, shed, a draw that
leads to cottonwoods. An immature cedar barrier runs between
this property and the McCleary's]

'Hey," he shouts, shaking a fist at you. "Care about me! Get out of your head and help! What's wrong with you, you oughta care about me!" With no time to spare, he jumps back to work.

[Backdrop: hard times. Drought conditions, low crop yields.
The farmer has persisted for seven years. His wife and
daughter are away tonight — thirty miles east. Alone, he
defends their food]
[Scene: farmer dragging long tarpaulins to save the cabbage]

A black sky releases the gray tonnage of pea-sized hail. The farmer curses, his dark figure cracks a sharp outline every time the lightning flashes. Something irritates him; in fact, he can't conceal the rage springing from his source of ruin. He continues to run from the barn, back and forth, dragging long tarpaulins. Strip by strip he covers their food-source, but it is a small area, nothing that will sustain the family. Everything is destroyed.

He rushes by, almost knocking you over.

```
[Scene: pea-size hail denuding all the foliage. Farmer is
desperate but continues to struggle. His crops are finished]
```

"This is my livelihood," he shouts at you. "What's wrong, why are you standin' there? You care nothing of a man's livelihood?" he thumps his chest. "Help a man in need!" His efforts are in vain. Devastation is total and he lumbers up the wooden steps to the back door and places a strong wet hand on your chest. "I've got a mind to set you straight," the farmer says with a shove. You stagger into the black, unlit house, stumbling over wooden planks. His boots rattle the floor. Water drips off the farmer in long stringy beads.

He sighs, discards the hat and kerchief, tossed carelessly in some unknown direction. Now alone, he sits quietly. Just sits. Minutes pass wordlessly. But the hail... it is loud. The roof creaks as the rafters bend, threatening to collapse. The tension torques into your shoulders, pulling them to ears.

Eventually, the storm abates. When it does, the weather's exit is immense. The silence is heavier than the ice-tonnage crushing the ground. He laughs, not much, but he must. To do nothing is folly. Despair.

"I fight six years against this drought, and when the water does come, it takes everything away." In the dark, the farmer grabs a steel canteen off the shelf and taps his fingers against the sawtooth edge. Then he takes a drink. "Warren." Warren wipes the corner of his mouth. His handshake is strong. Your knuckles and ligaments buckle into a circle under his grip.

"When did you show up? I coulda used your help to save what little bit of the crops. Can't for my life figure why you was doing nothing, standing idly in your head," he says, the voice hoarse. "No mind. S'pose I should turn on some light. No mind. No sense in turnin' on some light."

It feels rude to track water into the farmer's besieged home. A fine layer of dust covers the walls, vulnerable to the lightest breath.

"I s'pose this the human condition. We're not meant to know the minds 'o others. Still, it's a mean thing not to care." Warren takes another drink. "There's ah seat o'er in the corner. Sit if you please. Stay awhile. Roads'll be a mess tonight. I got some blankets and ah lie on the floor if you figure to take the master bed."

It's curious that Warren would sleep on the floor rather than his daughter's bed. Perhaps it is too small... or too fine a thing with its kewpie doll lying in the middle.

"Shoulda taken the govr'ment money for clover and alfalfa. Would be in a different position. That's what I get for principled matters s'pose. Lord tempts me and Lord keeps me. I have ah mind to head thirty miles to town and warm my'seln on a whiskey. He decrees it so but reminds us ah the troubles in rye. Besides, the missus would be sorrowful on this account."

You mean to say something but the lightning flickers silently revealing the home's interior in a white burst. Warren and his family don't have much. Perhaps he'll take interest in cards, something to get his mind off things. But the threat of violence looms. He has lost his livelihood and the missus is away. Besides, there's a morbid fascination in Warren's tone, like he means to sup on destruction.

"My livelihood," he barely mumbles. "Times come for the city, s'pose."

"No."

But he doesn't react.

"Insurance is woeful... our crooked bankers. I'll rather sell off my assets. Wonder whether my things might be worth more where'n you come from." He swallows another sip from the canteen and wipes his mouth with his wet sleeve. The distant rumble of thunder finally follows the lightning. "No mind. Go back to the city like my father. He was a nice real talker. I guess there's some ah him in me and I can go in insurance. Done it once already."

He taps the canteen, then sets it down.

"The missus folks got a place back in Chicago. Mr. Orlean say there's a spot for me." Warren shakes his head. "The lined is unkind."

The line or the land? You aren't quite sure.

"Imagine I make some mess o' money. Pay for a red cab and dress the missus in a white coat so long it drag on the ground. We'll smoke fine tobacco and see the opera, stay in the Waldorf where champagne is always cold. Then... I 'spect we'll crack lobster from the claw and shine our chins on a little warm butter."

Warren titters drunkenly although he hasn't consumed a drop.

"I'll be in the big screens."

"I've been meaning to talk to you about that," you say.

Pulled from his revery, Warren straightens up. "Oh? Where'n precisely resides your authority?"

"That's just it. Out *there*," you point. "I shouldn't be *here*."

"Oh? Suppose'n you tell me why."

"I made you. You're mine. A piece of imagination."

Warren lets out an unhappy sigh. It sounds as if he disagrees with this and is ready to deliver a thumping. "I think maybe you should reconsider your stance on account of facts."

You rub your hands upon your face and massage the tension. Cold water sits in your hair; chills run down the shoulders.

"Way I see it, Mr. Visitor... is I'm drowning in the ice, trying to save my family's food... and you watch over my shoulder without so much a hand to help. What am I to you?" he barks. "I am my brother's keeper, and should ever you find yourself confined to a similar predicament, I wouldn't likewise visit the same measure of cruelty on your condition..."

"But, Warren," you insist, "that's just the problem. You're not real. You're from my head."

Warren pounds his fist into the table. A bowl! A spoon! Something flies across the room, its contrail whizzes by your ear. "I *is* flesh and blood, same as you, sir!" he shouts. "Now, what do you mean this nonsense of being out of your head?"

You get up to stand at a spot farther away from Warren. "Warren," you say, with a notion that logic can restore clarity. "Your wife. Now, what is her name?"

He can't know. It hasn't been made.

"Clara. A fine piano player too. She performed concerts in Boston. That was many years ago. And my daughter. Cynthia. She plays in service every Sunday, twenty-eight miles from here. Overton. Yes. The fellowship loves her playing. My wife taught her. Voices too. A choir of angels, all stuffed inside two women. If you heard it, you wouldn'tah believe it."

It's touching. But not convincing. "Sounds lovely, Warren..."

"Why settle in civility? If I ain't real, there's no need to be mannered. Treat me like a dog if you please. What does it matter?"

Warren steps toward you, then lights a match. An oil lamp is in his hand. He ignites the orb, the circle of glass comes on like magic filling a pink bubble. With the lamp steady, he flings one of his oaken limbs in a huge windmill. You flinch.

"I thought you says I ain't real." He paces back and forth, then sets the lamp on the table.

Somewhat embarrassed, you notice your arms raised in protection, hands halfway open or clenched. "It appears I'm on your side," you say to enjoin a small conciliation.

Before you can dodge him, Warren is beside you, grabbing your arm. "Feel this?" The wet clothes, stuck to his body, pull off in a suction. He shakes you so hard your head whips about. It hurts. You fear he might breach restraint, that violence will win over fully the evening's destruction.

But Warren lets go and returns to his chair.

"What will you do?" you ask. Logic didn't work.

He titters again with that sober drunken sound. "I already says so. Join the silver screen and strike my face high off the wall for *aaaall* to see!"

You look at your hands under the faint glow in the room and see the accursed tools responsible for such harsh, lifeless stage directions. Being on the wrong side deprives you of your control. And there... in that condition... one is forced to confront the positivity of one's assumptions.

"Besides," Warren says, "I like for the missus to gwine play the real piano. I figure her talent lie too long under the burden of domestic confinement. She's a wonder, sir. I mean, a real angel. Sometimes... out in my fields, I bury my shamefulness in the soil. Clara had a society of gentlemen to choose. Do you know, sir, that her namesake comes from a famous musical German? You'll pardon my ignorance. The name escapes. But this man was married to a world famous piano concert-ist. A fine woman in her own right. She performed all over Europe."

Now: devised in your head, this man, Warren, was a brute. For certain, you've seen the edge, the tension, the sense for violence. But the catchphrase, 'domestic confinement.' There was nothing about him to be concerned about the opposite sex. As Warren drums his long, bony fingers upon the table in a clumsy, agitated rhythm, you bite your nails and squint.

"Maybe, I can get you out of here?" you say, pulling a seat from the table and sitting. The chair creaks... but holds.

"Out of here? No. I mean to go to Chicago. I already says Mr. Orlean has a place for me. I'll putter to his door, soggy hat in hand, and pin chin to chest in beseechment."

"You must fight on, Warren."

He stops his drumming. "Fight? I seen enough of that." Warren shakes his head. "Noooo," he mutters in reverence... drawing from the source of sacred memories. "Mr. Orlean said there wasn't no life to be found in an ocean of prairie. But I was born of mud, and in the soil, my heart lies content. I stays clear of violence and temptation. But yes... I think of Clara and her tolerance. I'm powerful lucky. Or blessed, s'pose."

There are moral considerations at play tonight. As the creator, you feel hopelessly drawn to discovery. Where has this gone wrong? "You seem fairly articulate, Warren.

I mean, the phrasing is a bit heckled, but the application of words belies intelligence. Where are you from? I'm trying to place it."

His brow hangs low to his eyes studying you from across the room. "That's supper talk, sir." Warren gets up, unclasps his overalls, and lets the straps hang down his legs. He pulls cold foods off the shelf by the sink, bread and salted meat wrapped in white grease paper. With each, he puts them on the table with exaggerated thuds. Warren tends to the coffee next, gets it going, and places two plates, silverware, napkins, and a jar with a red lid.

"That's to oil your bread," he says, wagging a finger at the thick grease inside the jar. "The missus spices it with a little pepper. Pray, you can abide."

He lights two more lamps on the wall which gives the room a low, even glow. Extinguishing the match, Warren resumes fetching supper. He drags a dozen glass jars to the table, a variety of preserved fruits and pickled wares. He finds two war-era tin cups and fills them with milk from the icebox. Just as you figure he's done, Warren returns to the icebox and produces a severed head of lamb, placing it on the table between the two of you. It's hard to ignore; the grinning teeth look like the sawtooth edge from the canteen.

"Everything is 'ah ruin," he winks. "You'll forgive my incivility tonight, but s'pose you'n help yourself."

With that, he opens lids and spears apricots and berries and vinegar-ed eggs and salted pork. Warren puts some in his mouth, some on his plate, bites the oiled bread with black flakes floating through the lard. He takes a giant swig of milk, the dense white substance dripping down the folds of his chin onto a stained shirt.

"Are you from Boston?" you ask.

He chews a mouthful of greased bread. "No."

"Your wife?"

"No. New Haven. I found her in Boston. After the war."

Politeness begs you to follow the conversation, but there is a lamb's head on the table; intact. Even the eyes. A blend of cooked muscle and threads gather your attention to the area between the empty nose and watchful eye. Warren slides a spoon down this spot scraping together a ball of succulent meat. He dumps it on his plate.

"I come from Georgia."

"Ah," you say. "What town?"

He shakes his head, chewing another lofty midden of oil-bread. The table's spread doesn't even smell like a meal. It's a garage odor, a mechanic's shop with all the grit, metal shavings, and axle grease. The opening of this interior world is troublesome. You have created none of it... and it doesn't meet expectations. The supper's scent undermines every conviction.

"No town, sir. I issued from the mud. Like I says, 'member?'"

"The mud," you say. No question in it. A quiet statement, to be honest.

In the background, what has been silence is replaced by rain. It is not of the previous temperament... with its heavy-handed destruction. A gentle peal of thunder lengthens the sky, flickers in the window, and rain begins gently to fuzz the roof.

"I spring from the mud of our creeks. The iniquity of the earth!" Warren winks again. He puts a pickled egg into his mouth, jabs a piece of salted pork, and wobbles it at you in accusation. As the sound of his gustation subsides, a matter that takes several minutes, he fashions an alternative perspective of the matter.

"If I rightly preside where'n you think I do, then our conference is a matter of grave concern."

"I agree, Warren."

"And the issue of who's partic'ler ground we stand 'pon."

Before you can say a thing, he interrupts.

"I notice you haven't eaten a bite. Is the spread not to your liking?"

"They are, Warren," and you, with hand pressed to the table, seek to communicate his error. "You only saw me after I fell through the sheets of time." The chair creaks when you shift.

He smiles. "I like that. Pleases the ear," and Warren repeats the phrase, "Sheets 'o time."

To appease the host, you dive a fork into the jar with apricots and pull out two. "And till that point, I planned on designing your success... uh, you know, after the storm. A bank seizure of assets or something. A family member you didn't know about. And there's some kind of antiquity on the property. And, it's yours. And it's valuable. Perhaps a gold pocket watch stowed behind a brick in the hearth."

'He raises an eyebrow, "Oh?"

"Yes. I mean, to me, you *are* the hero."

Warren titters again. "Hero!" He shakes his head. "No, sir. And come to prove how little you know me... and much apologies for discontenting your view... but, a stack o' money, or fortune would do me no good. I would'na want bedevilments such as that! No sir. I knows my'seln better 'an you... and you can stuff that in your head for here till eternity. Any good fortune to me must be righteous and earned. No sir! A stack of money would put me in the cement'ry... I know what rightly I'd do with that. There'd be sorrow on account of the missus, for surely my sinful nature would be unleashed." Warren goes to fetch the coffee. He fills two more metal cups. "Maybe the coffee is more to your liking." He holds it out, but the metal is too hot to touch.

Observing, Warren sets it on the table. You lean forward to sniff the steam, circumspect now of any foodstuff. He turns in time to see you flaring the nostrils exactly as a small mammal would do. The gesture is obvious, your effrontery to graciousness and mild manners easy to interpret. When in this home, you ought to do as your mother taught. But he chooses not to say a thing, rather the mutual understanding about this rudeness is enough. Warren knows it and sits down.

Those teeth from the lamb's head stare back at you. The coffee smells all right, but again, it mingles with the automotive quality of the room. That, paired with the molars and canines, offsets any pretension to coffee.

"If you left me well enough alone, Warren, I could've saved your crops. Your livelihood."

"Would you have?" Warren daubs a napkin to his face but fails to clean his greasy chin. He goes back for more, stacking layers of salt pork and scraping new balls of lamb's head.

He waits for an answer; your honesty, however, dies torturously in the sinews.

"No. Don't s'pose you would," he affirms. "That crop decimation is vital to your organs. I mean... it's something you have to have. And what am I to you but an idea? Yet! Here I sit, we break bread together, we grow fat off my ruin... draining my larders ah finest wares. Yet I bleed, sir," he whacks the table. Coffee and milk splatter out the cups. "I bleed!"

You nod, studying the blackened char upon the lamb's teeth.

"And you'll allow me this remark," he announces with that accusatory fork, "You, sir... are not one for facts. Yes! That's correct. I believe it to the soul. You are *not* a man of facts!"

The temerity of his declaration gathers all your focus onto the glistening marvel of his shining chin. You wish that he might wipe it clean. His failure to do so reminds you of childhood, of trying to find the itching spot on your back, scratching, scratching, feeling your efforts close in on it without ever getting there.

"If we have no facts," you say, "then we have nothing."

But he has a point. This man, this farmer; you can't precisely define his being. Certainly, he has a mother. No one is birthed from catfish mud-holes.

Warren swallows, "God, grant me mercy, for judgment comes like a thief in night, or labor pains 'pon the expectant mother."

A gentle peal of thunder rolls over the prairie, its sound muted by the velvet rain. You look out the window, but it is only a square of black glass.

"It's cold in here," you say.

Warren readies another piece of bread with an over-portioned wad of oil. "Yes, sir. A ghost gwine through the room. Settle here to make 'is home."

"Ghost?" You think about his statement of *facts*.

"She come around. She from the war."

"There's no such thing, Warren."

He bites half the bread-piece and chews, A smirk develops on his stuffed face. Warren winks. "The war?"

"Ghosts. Ghosts. There's no such thing."

He knows what you mean. That's evident by his smile. "She does, sir. Reminds me 'o things. Tell me why no harm I oughta visit 'pon those who watch others suffer. No sir! We are all conformed in the image and likeness of our creator. You know what I thought as you stood on my porch watching me cover my cabbages? Why, I thought, this man should die for his sin. Lord, let me be your instrument of peace. Lord, let me be your instrument of justice. Lord, let me be your instrument of retribution... so that I might render 'pon the wicked your righteous designs. And the Lord spoke to me. You know what he says? He says, Warren, it is for *me alone* to give and to take. It is for *you* to serve. The man on your porch is ig'nornt and a-feared. And I will use you to bring him into my house."

You look around Warren's home.

He laughs. "This ain't it!"

Chastened, you clutch the table, examine the coffee. The oils in the house are not as offensive now. "There was a moment..."

"A moment of surrender?"

You shake your head. "Where I thought you were meaning to kill me."

The laughing vanishes. "I shall do as he commands."

This leaves the room flat, and you reflect on sleeping tonight in his home... in the master's bed. Being dissolved into language, you weep. Your palms and fingers turn wet with tears; home is so far away. Perhaps this man, Warren, is on the wrong side and you can offer to pull him through the sheets 'o time.

A hand clutches your shoulder. You jump. Warren is there, then gets down on a knee. "I don't let the missus see me, nor my Cynthia. But I steal into the potato cellar, where it's always cool, and cry in my hands. I believe the Lord is in our hands."

Up close, his face is homely, pale. The chin shines and teeth chatter. If he doesn't get out of those freezing clothes, Warren will surely catch deep dark sick. Then you notice despite him kneeling, your faces are even. You look to your hands and see they are the tender, smooth ones of a child. The words have been stealing flesh and bone; the malady of linguistic diminution. Letters swirl away in tiles, spinning off like children discarded from a merry-go-round.

A breeze carries through the kitchen and all the oil lamps warble in a dance. The light flickers from yellow to pink to yellow. Warren hugs you, because like the child after a stormy temper; whimpers and quivers shake your body.

He is cold.

"I think I'll sleep in Cynthia's bed," you say, "In the corner."

Warren pats your shoulder. "My apologies on account of supper. I don't s'pose none of it was to your liking." He lifts the cup of milk. "At least drink this."

You do. And it's good.

"I fear my waste has become yours," he says. "But, at least I can putter back to the city. Things will turn 'round." Warren stands up quickly. "My God, You're but a field mouse."

The house has grown immense and the rafters look far away. The only thing which hasn't changed is the gentle thunder and the patter of rain. The sound is comforting.

"Warren," you say.

He bends down and presents an ear.

"Use my napkin. Please! Wipe your chin. It'll go up in flames."

He pats his shirt, forgetting his overalls hang down his legs, looking for a kerchief. Then he picks up your unused napkin and applies it vigorously to the chin. When he is done, Warren smiles for inspection.

It's no use. The chin positively glows. By now, it is nearly as bright as the lamps on the wall, a center collecting Warren's thoughts into a mass of lead. But it's not collecting his thoughts, you think, *it is collecting mine.*

"Are you still sad?" he asks.

"Yes." And it's true, you are. *Why?* And then you realize that is to do with his farm. All the food. All that livelihood you took away. "I don't know."

Warren picks you up in the palm of his hands and carries you to Cynthia's bed. He shakes his head, "Still not one for facts," and places you in the center beside his child's kewpie doll. The toy's eyes stare happily into nowhere. "If you pardon me, I'll fetch one of the missus' scarves. It will provide warmth and comfort."

He leaves you alone in Cynthia's bed beside her kewpie. As you admire the toy, as big as you are, he returns with the loveliest, brightest red scarf you've ever seen. Warren lays it around in a circle, taking one end to cover your body. The scarf smells like the sun... and pollen... a blend of citrus and leather promising puffiness behind your eyes. Warren's attention is fastidious, and it pleases him, so he starts to hum.

```
[Set: The home's interior transitions back and forth between
pink and yellow. Occasional thunder is seen in the kitchen
window. The sound of soothing rain is heard around the
audience]
```

"Well, Mr. Visitor... perhaps I can please you with a story. Being one against facts, I s'pose'n you relish in the trickeration of words."

You nod.

He leans close and uses his giant finger to stroke your hair. "It's okay. Please hear me, Mr. Visitor. I know your sadness. It's the sin of living that makes it hard to live."

You nod. By tomorrow, you'll have aromatized into a world you no longer control, and that's the only fact you can get your head around.

Instead of a story, Warren sings a song, something old from the cave walls of ancient humanity; straight from the fires and midnights that penetrate in knives to the deepest sets of the skull. The lamb head continues to stare from the table, an entoptic pattern of molars, canines, and incisors. The flesh about its nose is gone.

The songs don't put you to sleep, but they take the worry away. With a smile, he stands up.

"I need to 'spect the damage to the property." He grabs the overall straps and reaffixes them on his shoulder, clasping the buttons into the irons. In contradiction to the mournful melodies he just sang, Warren now whistles a happy tune. "All this may be a flight 'o fancy. The insurance will spare us some..." his words trail off into the night as he exits through the back door.

[Scene: you lay beside the kewpie doll, swaddled by the red scarf, as befitting man and wife.
[Sound: rain and thunder continue to permeate the audience. They wait for it to end. It goes on]

CONTRIBUTORS' NOTES

Derek Annis is the author of Neighborhood of Gray Houses (Lost Horse Press), and the manager of the Blue Lynx Prize for Poetry, an annual full-length poetry collection contest run by Lynx House Press. They are also the Lynx House Press social media manager. Their poems have appeared in *The Account*, *Colorado Review*, *Epiphany*, *The Gettysburg Review*, *The Missouri Review Online*, *Spillway*, *Third Coast*, and many other journals. To find out more, visit derekannis.wordpress.com.

Aaron Anstett's new and selected poems, *This Way to the Grand As-Is*, was published nearly simultaneously with the world-wide pandemic lockdown. You could delight his publisher by buying a copy. Days, Anstett writes and edits technical documents. Nights, he expands his cooking repertoire and listens to skronky, arduous music on headphones to spare his beloved, Lesley.

Gregory Ariail lives and teaches in Tuscaloosa, Alabama. His work has appeared in *Indiana Review*, *DIAGRAM*, *The Common*, *The Offing*, and others.

M. C. Aster's writing reflects her varied biography: born in Yugoslavia, life in Ethiopia during formative years, and work in Europe. Aster's poems have appeared in *Slipstream, Meat for Tea/The Valley Review*, the *Stonecrop Review*, and in *Poeming Pigeon's Cosmos Issue* (February 2020). Aster is currently working on a speculative short story collection, as well as some new poetry. Aster lives in Mentone, California, where she fosters two endangered desert tortoises.

Simon Anton Nino Diego Baena's poems have appeared in *The Cortland Review, Fifth Wednesday*, and *North Dakota Quarterly*, among others. He also has a chapbook out, from Jacar Press, *The Magnum Opus Persists in the Evening*, and publishes the online poetry journal, *January Review.*

Rebecca Berg works as a cello teacher and a freelance editor, and she is on the faculty of the Lighthouse Writers Workshop in Denver. Her fiction has appeared or is forthcoming in *Chicago Review*, *Five Fingers Review, Four Way Review, Map Literary, Midwestern Gothic, Still Point Arts Quarterly, Water-Stone Review*, and *Word Riot.*

Jacob Bingham is an Appalachian writer who earned his MFA at the Bluegrass Writers Studio through Eastern Kentucky University. He seeks to create authentic representations of Appalachia to combat the stereotypes and exploitation the region constantly battles. His short fiction has been published online in *Light and Dark Magazine.*

Jacob Chapman lives in Amherst, MA with his wife and daughter. His chapbook *Other Places* was chosen as the winner of the Open Country Press Chapbook Prize by Michael Earl Craig.

Nicoletta Ceccoli was born and still lives in her native Republic of San Marino. She graduated from the State Institute of Art in Urbino (Italy) in animation. An illustrator of children's books since 1995, she has illustrated numerous books with U.S., U.K., Italian, Swiss, and Taiwanese publishers. Her clients include Random House, Mondadori, Simon and Schuster, Barefoot Books, Fabbri, Arka, Fatatrac, EuropaCorp, Macy's, Houghton Mifflin, Henry Holt, United Airlines, and Vogue. Her many awards include the Andersen Prize "Baia della favole" as best illustrator of the year in Italy and a Silver Medal from the Society of illustrators of New York.

Stephen Delaney writes fiction, craft articles, and book reviews. His work has been featured in, among other places, *Crazyhorse, Euphony, New World Writing, Requited, Gingerbread House*, and *Tahoma Literary Review*.

Tudor Evans has worked in education, the criminal justice system, and The British Film Industry, and throughout it all, he has been involved in developing surrealist ideas and projects. Rather than computer technology or photocopies, Tudor uses traditional cut and paste methods, original 19th century engravings from Victorian books and magazines, scissors, and occasionally scalpels! His collages reflect on contemporary society and are often set in dystopian worlds; they comment on imperialism, organised religion, and the roles of men and women through the prism of select 19th century engravings.

As an artist, **Daniel Ferris** creates within and around the medium of abstract conception, including fantasy creatures and otherworldly settings. Originally working only in pencil and ink, he has more recently begun an exploration into the world of digital creation. He currently lives on the outskirts of Olympia, Washington.

Peter Grandbois is the author of eleven books, the most recent of which is the poetry collection The Three-Legged World, published in a Triptych edition with books by James McCorkle and Robert Miltner (Etruscan 2020). His work has appeared in over one hundred journals, including *The Kenyon Review*, *The Gettysburg Review*, and *Prairie Schooner*. His plays have been performed in St. Louis, Columbus, Los Angeles, and New York. He is a senior editor at *Boulevard magazine* and teaches at Denison University in Ohio. You can find him at www.petergrandbois.com.

Jenny Grassl was raised in Pennsylvania, and now lives in Cambridge, Massachusetts. Her poems appeared in *The Boston Review* 2018 annual poetry contest, runner-up prize selected by Mary Jo Bang. In 2019, the anthology *Humanagerie, Eibonvale Press, UK, Rhino Poetry, Phantom Drift, Radar Poetry*, and *The Massachusetts Review* published her work. Her poems are forthcoming in *Lily Poetry Review* and *Inverted Syntax*.

Jonathan Greenhause, winner of Aesthetica Magazine's 2018 Creative Writing Award in Poetry, was also shortlisted for this year's Mick Imlah Poetry Prize from London's Times Literary Supplement. His poems have recently appeared or are forthcoming in *New Ohio Review, Notre Dame Review, Salamander*, and The Poetry Society website, among others.

Samarah Greeves attended the University of Iowa, where she was fortunate to have poetry writing workshops with Marvin Bell, James Galvin, and Jorie Graham. She took a detour from writing to pursue her Master's in Social Work and currently works as a mental health therapist. Samarah is currently working on a novel along with writing poetry.

Lesley Hart Gunn, from Nova Scotia, Canada, currently resides in Utah with her partner and children, teaching academic writing.

Lily Hoang is an associate professor of Creative Writing at UC-San Diego and the author of five books of prose, including *Changing* (recipient of a PEN Open Books Award) and *A Bestiary* (winner of the Cleveland State University Poetry Center's Non-Fiction Book Prize). With Joshua Marie Wilkinson, she edited the anthology *The Force of What's Possible: Writers on Accessibility and the Avant-Garde*. In Summer 2017, she was Mellon Scholar in Residence at Rhodes University in South Africa. She is Editor of Jaded Ibis Press and Executive Editor of HTML Giant.

Elizabeth Howard earned an MFA in Poetry at Boston University, and currently lives in the forests of Eugene, where she is working towards her PhD in Comparative Literature at the University of Oregon. She writes poetry and fiction inspired by myth and folklore. Elizabeth will never refuse a freshly buttered piece of toast.

Sarah Kain Gutowski is the author of *Fabulous Beast: Poems* (Texas Review Press), runner-up for the 2018 X.J. Kennedy Prize, winner of the 14th annual National Indie Excellence Award for Poetry, and a 2019 Foreword INDIES Finalist. She is also the author of a chapbook, *Fabulous Beast: The Sow*, published by Hyacinth Girl Press. She holds an MFA in poetry from New York University and a BA from James Madison University. Her poems have appeared in various print and online journals, including *The Threepenny Review, So To Speak: A Feminist Journal of Language and Art, Painted Bride Quarterly, The Gettysburg Review*, and *The Southern Review*. As a professor of English at Suffolk County Community College, she has co-chaired the annual SCCC Creative Writing Festival for over a decade.

Stories and poems by **Ray Keifetz** have appeared in the Ashland Creek Press, *The Bitter Oleander, Briar Cliff Review, Heartland Review, Kestrel, The Louisville Review* and others. His debut poetry collection "Night Farming In Bosnia" won the Bitter Oleander Press Library of Poetry award in 2017.

Stacey Levine is the author of four books of fiction. Her story collection *THE GIRL WITH BROWN FUR*, which was longlisted for The Story Prize, was also shortlisted for the Washington State Book Award in 2012. Her novel *FRANCES JOHNSON* was shortlisted for the Washington State Book Award in 2005, and her collection *MY HORSE AND OTHER STORIES* won a PEN/West Fiction Award. *MY HORSE* and Levine's novel *DRA—* were published by the much-lauded Sun & Moon Press in the 1990s. A Pushcart Prize nominee, her fiction has appeared in the *Denver Quarterly, Fence, Tin House, The Fairy Tale Review, The Iowa Review, The Notre Dame Review, Yeti*, and other venues. Levine received a Stranger Genius Award for Literature in 2009 and her fiction has been translated for Japanese and Danish publications.

John Lewis's fiction has appeared in *Spry Literary Journal* and *Chantwood Magazine*. He co-founded *The Almagre Review*, a Colorado publication, and helped run it for three years. He has a degree in art, and by day works in a laboratory monitoring water quality all over the State of Colorado.

Julia Lillard is a self-taught digital collage artist who lives and works in Oklahoma City, Oklahoma. She was born in Hereford, Texas, in 1955 and moved with her family to Oklahoma when she was a child. Julia's artworks look pretty gloomy, sometimes very mysterious, or utterly frightening. Some of her work echoes the elegant surrealism of Max Ernst and yet, her work somehow transcends Surrealism, is almost a new visual portrayal of the Human, amalgamating the physical and spiritual realms all at once in a kind of breathtakingly heightened awareness. Julia's artwork has been shown in exhibitions in Oklahoma City and Palermo, Italy, as well as in several publications including *The September Issues*, *V magazine*, *CyberZone*, and many others as well.

Rebecca Lilly works as a writer, photographer, field assistant to a landscape architect, and guest lecturer. She holds degrees from Cornell (M.F.A., poetry) and Princeton (Ph.D., philosophy) Universities and has published several collections of poems, including two gift books of haiku—one collection on butterflies (*A Prism of Wings*) and a companion volume on wildflowers (*Light's Reservoir*)—each featuring twelve color plates of specimens by recognized artists. Her poetry has appeared widely in national magazines and literary journals. Her latest collection is *Creatures Among Us*. You may find her at RebeccaLilly.com.

Bruce McAllister's fiction has appeared in literary magazines like GLIMMER TRAIN and IMAGE and his short SFF&H fiction has appeared over the years in various magazines in the field, theme anthologies, and "year's best" volumes. His most recent novel, fabulist as well, was *THE VILLAGE SANG TO THE SEA: A MEMOIR OF MAGIC*.

Benjamin Niespodziany is a Pushcart Prize nominee with work in *Fairy Tale Review*, *Hobart*, *Paper Darts*, *Peach Mag*, and various others. He works in a library in Chicago and runs the multimedia platform [neonpajamas].

Peter O'Donovan is a scientist and writer living in Seattle, WA. Originally from Saskatchewan, he received his doctorate in Computer Science from the University of Toronto, with a focus on design aesthetics. His poetry has appeared or is forthcoming in *Typehouse Magazine*, *Sheila-Na-Gig*, *Qwerty*, and *the Torontoist*.

Steven Owen has a PhD in creative writing and literature from the University of Utah, and an MFA from Notre Dame in prose. He has worked as an editor at the Notre Dame Review, flatmancrooked, and mixer publishing. His stories investigate the limits of human empathy and impossible realism.

Adam Penna is the author of *Little Songs & Lyrics to Genji*, *The Love of a Sleeper*, *Small Fires, Little Flames and Talk of Happiness*. He is a Professor of English at Suffolk County Community College and lives in East Moriches with his family.

"The Marionettes" is **John Pospichal**'s first published story. He is a graduate of South Florida University with a B.A. in English.

Natanya Ann Pulley is a Diné writer and her clans are Kinyaa'áani (Towering House People) and Tǎchii'nii (Red Running into Water People). She's published in *Waxwing*, *Monkeybicycle*, *SplitLip*, and *The Offing* (among others). Natanya is the founding editor of Hairstreak Butterfly Review and teaches texts by Native American writers, Fiction Writing, and Experimental Forms at Colorado College. Her debut story collection *With Teeth* was published by New Rivers Press (Oct. 2019) and her writing can be found at natanyapulley.com.

Katie Quarles has a B.A. in Literature from U.C. Santa Cruz. She was the recipient of the 2008 Ina Coolbrith Memorial Prize. Her work has appeared in numerous journals including *Apocryphal Text*, *Inter|rupture*, *Poetry Now*, *Dime Show Review*, and the anthology *Connoisseurs of Suffering*. She works as a freelance copyeditor in Rocklin, California.

Portland poet **dan raphael**, has had two new books published this year: Starting Small (his 24th book) came out in October from Alien Buddha Press and Moving with Every was published in June by Flowstone Press. Most Wednesdays dan writes and records a current events poem for The KBOO Evening News.

Melissa Reddish's fiction has appeared in *decomP*, *Prick of the Spindle*, and *Gargoyle*, and in a recent collection of stories entitled *My Father is an Angry Storm Cloud* (Tailwinds Press, 2016) and novella entitled *Girl & Flame* (Conium Books, 2017). She has received residencies at Soaring Gardens and the Rensing Center.

Kyle Rowland is a writer, poet, and essayist propelled by travel, punk rock, and an irrational phobia of cubicles and neck ties. He is working on a series of "cli-fi" stories set in American West while hammering away at a Masters of Fine Arts degree at Eastern Oregon University, and has poems appearing in *The Sierra Nevada Review*. Nowadays, he can be found hunting the seemingly small detail that reveals a poem, or following the strand that leads to a compelling narrative. He lives in Silverton, Oregon with his wife Jennifer and a small coven of black cats.

Matt Schumacher's prose poetry collection, *A Missing Suspiria de Profundis*, was published in Summer 2019 by Greying Ghost Press. Previous poetry collections include the titles *Spilling the Moon*, *The Fire Diaries*, *Ghost Town Odes*, and *favorite maritime drinking songs of the miraculous alcoholics*. Recent poems have appeared in *The Journal*, *Birdcoat Quarterly*, and *Bombay Gin*. Matt lives in Portland, Oregon, with his beloved, Kaley, and several pampered rescued animals.

Michael Stein is a writer and journalist in the Czech Republic and has published short stories and journalism with a number of European and American magazines. He runs a website on Central European writing called Literalab and has written for literary journals such as *Asymptote* and the *The Review of Contemporary Fiction*. He is an editor at the Prague-based journal B O D Y and runs the Saturday European Fiction series. His own fiction has been published in *The Missing Slate* and *McSweeney's,* among other magazines.

David Surface has stories published in *Shadows & Tall Trees*, *Supernatural Tales*, *Darkest Minds*, and his first collection, *Terrible Things*, was recently published by Black Shuck Books.

Kailey Tedesco is the author of *She Used to be on a Milk Carton* (April Gloaming Publishing) and *Lizzie, Speak* (winner of White Stag Publishing's 2018 MS contest). Her newest collection, FOREVERHAUS, will be released from White Stag in 2020. She is a senior editor for Luna Luna Magazine, and she teaches an ongoing course on the witch in literature at Moravian College. You can find her work featured or forthcoming in *Electric Literature*, *Black Warrior Review*, *Gigantic Sequins*, *Blood Bath Zine*, *Fairy Tale Review*, and more. For further information, please follow @kaileytedesco.

Cindy Veach is the author of *Her Kind* (CavanKerry Press, forthcoming) and *Gloved Against Blood* (CavanKerry Press), named a finalist for the Paterson Poetry Prize and a 'Must Read' by The Massachusetts Center for the Book. Her poems have appeared in the Academy of American Poets Poem-a-Day Series, *AGNI, Prairie Schooner, Poet Lore, Michigan Quarterly Review, Diode* and elsewhere. She received the 2019 Phillip Booth Poetry Prize and the 2018 Samuel Allen Washington Prize. Cindy is co-poetry editor of *Mom Egg Review*. www.cindyveach.com

Cynthia Zhang is a writer, scholar, and dog aficionado currently based in Los Angeles, where she is currently a Ph.D. student at the University of Southern California. Among other venues, her work has appeared in *Leading Edge, Coffin Bell, Lunch Ticket*, and *Orca, A Literary Journal*. Her first novel, *After the Dragons*, is forthcoming in 2021 with Stelliform Press.

Accepting Submissions for Issue No. 11
January 1 - April 30, 2021

Please read guidelines carefully before submitting, then submit your fabulist story, poem, or critical essay for Issue #11 through our website at:
www.phantomdrift.org

Fiction:
$5 per page (minimum $10)

Poetry:
$5 per page (minimum $10)

Nonfiction:
$5 per page (minimum $10)

WE AT
PHANTOM DRIFT

GIVE A MONSTROUS

SHOUTOUT

TO CONTRIBUTORS,
DONORS AND
SUBSCRIBERS,
FOR BELIEVING IN US.
WE COULDN'T MANIFEST
WITHOUT YOU.

THANKS!!!

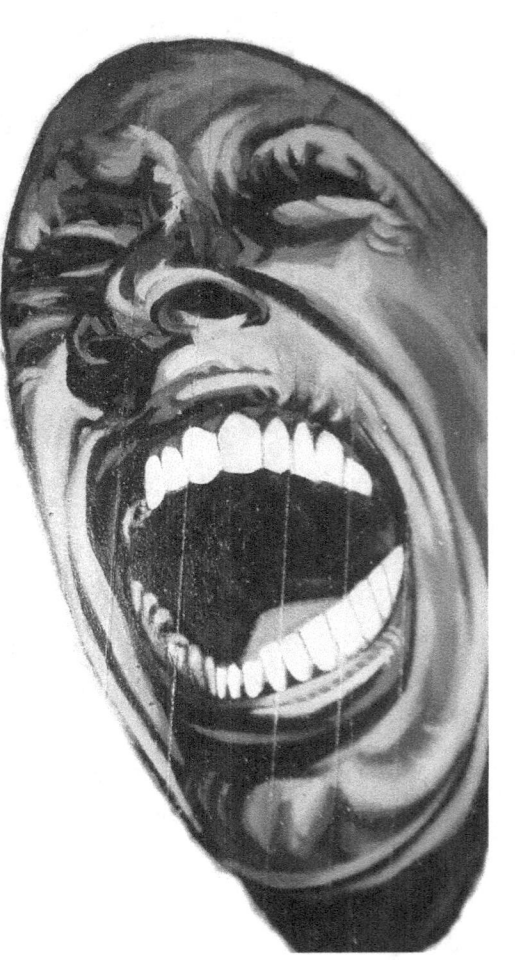

www.ingramcontent.com/pod-product-compliance
Lightning Source LLC
Chambersburg PA
CBHW080819250626
47159CB00011B/3446